I0713632

CYNTHIA HICKEY

SKIN CARE CAN BE MURDER

A Nosy Neighbor Mystery, Book 3

Cynthia Hickey

Copyright 2015
Written by: Cynthia Hickey
Published by: Winged Publications
Cover Design: Cynthia Hickey

This book is a work of fiction. Names, characters, places, and incidents are the product of the author's imagination and are used fictitiously. Any resemblance to actual events, locales, or persons, living or dead, is coincidental.

No part of this book may be copied or distributed without the author's consent.

ISBN-13: 978-1-962168-11-3

DEDICATION

To God for the never-ending ideas,
To my husband for his support and patience while I put
aside other duties to finish my latest novel,
And to my fans who keep wanting more.

1

"I'm going to make the world a more beautiful place." Angela plopped a giant pink chest, painted with white polka dots, onto the kitchen table.

I grabbed my glass of diet soda before she could knock it over. "You finally got your kit."

"I'm going to be rich in no time." She opened the chest to reveal trays and trays of beauty products ranging from makeup in every shade imaginable to face creams and body lotions. "You'll be my first customer. I really wish you would have booked a party for me. It's the least you could have done for your big sister."

A big pain in the rear was more like it. "I thought Norma Winston booked a party."

Angela frowned. "She signed up for this Friday, but you know most of the women who show up will be … well, you know," she lowered her voice. "Streetwalkers. I'll feel out of place."

"They probably use more makeup than anyone." I eyed her tight strapless dress and strappy sandals. She wouldn't look as out of place at Norma's as she thought.

I finished my soda and reached for the newspaper. Why Mom insisted on paying for the paper when we could easily read the news on the computer was beyond me, but since it sat here every morning, I'd read it. "Besides, Norma left that life behind her a long time ago."

Now, she made her money writing fan fiction, and not

1

doing too bad. After I'd suspected her of murder a few months ago, we'd become fast friends and her son gave me free coffee at the local coffee house. Life was good.

My first romantic mystery was still in the top five best sellers and the newly released novella, *A Killer Plot*,was climbing the ladder quickly. All I needed now was to come up with the plot of my third book, a full-length novel, I hoped. And hopefully, without a real live mystery that would almost get me killed in order for me to do research. Although, I did admit to missing the adrenaline rush of gathering clues and outsmarting a killer.

"You will come, won't you?"

"To the party? Of course." I scanned the front page of the newspaper, saw nothing to attract my attention and possibly form a book after, and set the paper aside. "I could use some … cream of some kind." Not really. I wore minimal makeup and avoided the sun at all costs. Being a redhead, the sun was not my friend.

"Wonderful, because I'm going to use you to demonstrate on." She grinned, closed her case, and then headed to her bedroom, tossing over her shoulder that she wished the work crew would speed things up on finishing her attic apartment.

Yikes. With my sensitive skin, I could only hope the new products wouldn't give me a rash in front of a crowd of women.

Banging from the third floor meant the contractors were hard at work turning my attic into Angela's private abode. My niece and nephew, Cherokee and Dakota, had opted to sleep in the main house with me. Another set of contractors was scheduled to begin work on the basement in the morning to provide an apartment for Mom.

I shook my head. Less than a year ago, I'd lived the hermit life of a romance novelist who was timid around people. Now, I had a dog, two cats, a houseful of family, a best friend, and the most wonderful boyfriend in the world. When my literary agent had told me to get out and mingle with the living more, I doubt even she expected this.

Angela thundered back down the stairs. "Emergency! Norma requested her Pink Lady Party be moved to tonight." She glanced at the clock. "In an hour! Get dressed. You're driving."

Ugh. I rolled my eyes and pushed away from my chair. "Mom!" I peered down the basement steps. "Angela's party got changed to now."

"For Pete's sake." She stomped up the stairs. "How am I going to get your basement packed up if I have to go buy facial cream?" She shook her head. "We can't leave the workers here alone. I'll have to meet you there. I won't be but a half hour late, if that. By the time she gets set up and stuff, I'll be knocking on the door. The guests most likely won't even be there by then."

"Sounds good." I raced to my room and pulled a blouse from my closet. Angela might let me wear jeans, but the tee shirt was out of the question. I dropped the tee in the clothes hamper and buttoned the royal blue blouse over my body. A quick swipe of the hair brush, then a quick updo of my hair, secured with a clip, and I was ready to be smeared with facial products.

With Thanksgiving behind us, and Christmas fast approaching, maybe I could purchase some items for my mother and niece as gifts. Of course, since Angela was selling the stuff, that's probably what we'd all get. I'd have to think of something else.

Angela waited in the car. I set the house alarm and bolted into the chilly winter air. I slid behind the wheel of my Mercedes. "I should have given you the keys to warm up the car."

"I don't want my makeup to melt." She hugged the pink

and white case.

"You can put it in the backseat," I said, backing out of the driveway. "It'll be fine. You can even put the seat belt around it."

"I realize you may think this is all funny, but I can really make a ton of money selling these products. Since this is my first party, I don't intend to let anything bad happen." She lifted her chin and stared out the window.

She could be uncomfortable if she wanted to. We drove in silence to Norma's house and pulled into the driveway of her modest ranch-style home. An older model Toyota, the brown paint long since oxidized, occupied the single car carport.

"This is *not* a good neighborhood," Angela stated, keeping a firm grip on her case and trying to get out of the car without letting go.

"It's all Norma can afford. Living a lawful law doesn't always pay." I yanked the case out of her hands. "I'll give it back when you get out of the car. Otherwise, you'll show those gang members what God intended for you to keep hidden."

She gasped, slid from the car, keeping her legs as modestly together as her spandex dress would allow, then took the case back. I slid out, locking the vehicle behind me. I tossed a wave to the young man lounging on the porch of the house next door. "Hey, Jamal!"

"Back at ya, Miss Stormi." He gave me a nod.

"You know gang members?" Angela asked in a hoarse whisper.

"I come here often enough to visit Norma, I thought I should at least meet the neighbors." The young men who considered the neighborhood their territory wouldn't mess with me as long as they considered me their friend.

"Are you bringing Norma another girl?"

"What does he mean?" Angela tottered on her heels. "I am

not one of Norma's girls. I thought you said she didn't have that life anymore."

"She doesn't. She works with prostitutes to try and bring them out of that lifestyle." I rapped on Norma's cheery red door. "Stop being such a snob."

"You sure have changed. What happened to my shy, reclusive sister?"

"She died right along with the first dead body I stumbled over." I grinned when Norma opened the door, wearing the same dress as Angela's blue one except hers was in a bright shade of red.

Angela groaned and entered the small but spotless home and set her case on the kitchen table. She glanced at the counter where finger sandwiches and fruit were arrayed on platters and mumbled something about appearances being deceiving.

I met Norma's amused glance and chose a chair next to the table in which to sit. "How many women are coming?"

"Five, not counting you and yours." Norma sat across from me. "Hookers like makeup and creams. Anything to make them feel pretty. I'm hoping that get-togethers like tonight will take them one step closer to realizing how cherished they are and that there are other career paths they can choose."

That got Angela's attention. She grinned. "Maybe I can sign one of them under me at this party. That will give you a huge discount."

Norma shrugged. "Anything's possible. Just don't push too hard, okay?"

"I'll present the facts as clearly as possible."

"I'm here!" Mom rushed through the front door, slamming it behind her. "Why is that young man always sitting outside giving the dog-eye to everyone who comes around?"

"Dog-eye?" I asked.

"Isn't that what they call that intense stare?" Mom plopped her purse on the floor behind the table. "I made it before the party. At least I hope we aren't the only guests."

"You aren't." Norma peered out her curtains, then reopened the door. "The girls are here."

"This is Ivy." She introduced an Amazon with the darkest skin I'd ever seen. Still, the woman's exotic beauty was definitely eye-catching. I was sure she charged a pretty penny. "This is Daisy," she said of a petite blond with too much pink makeup. Ginger was a redhead, except I guessed her particular shade came out of a bottle. Lacey, with ebony hair that fell to her waist, and Sissy, another African American girl with ample curves and dazzling white teeth, entered last and took their seats, all chattering like a group of school girls.

The amount of flesh showing in the room would have left a teenage boy grinning for weeks. I prayed double time for Norma's vision of bringing her friends into the light would come to fruition.

Angela clapped her hands. "Now that we are all here, I'd like to start my demonstration." She handed each woman a white cylinder. "After you wash off your makeup, of course, we'll fill these cylinders from this white pail," she motioned to a plastic container on the table, "and then let the mask set while we fill our plates with delicious finger foods."

The women made a mad dash to the one and only restroom and fought over the sink as they tried to rub off several layers of makeup.

"I should have told them to come paint free," Norma laughed. "I'll wash my face in the kitchen sink."

"I'm eating first," Sissy declared, as soon as she emerged from the bathroom. Soon, cylinders forgotten on the coffee table, everyone, including myself, crowded into the tiny kitchen.

Plates full, we pacified a pouting Angela by filling our cylinders and then smearing our faces with a pink cream that quickly dried on our skin. Despite my growling stomach, within seconds my face itched so bad, I could hardly concentrate on what I wanted to eat.

"Is it supposed to itch?" Ivy asked.

"Well, washing your face right before applying the cream did open your pores," Angela explained. "It's probably just working better than it would otherwise. Don't worry. Your skin will be as smooth as a baby's bottom when we're done."

Ivy peered closely at Daisy's face and scraped away a portion of the cream. "It looks more like a baby's bottom with diaper rash."

Angela shrieked and grabbed a cloth from a package of baby wipes that she had brought along. "She must be allergic to something in the cream. This cream is supposed to be hypoallergenic."

"I'm having a bit of trouble breathing," Daisy admitted.

"Somebody get her some water!" Tears streamed down Angela's face.

I scratched my fingernails down my cheeks, noticing that others were doing the same. We all looked like Daisy. Our faces were covered with a red, itchy rash.

Daisy fell to the floor, her hands grabbing at her throat. Her fine-boned face had swollen to almost twice its size. Heavens. Did we all look like that? I glanced around. No, just blotchy. Something had gone horribly wrong.

"Hurry, Angela." I grabbed another wipe. "Get this stuff off of her. Someone call 9-1-1."

"They're coming," Sissy said.

Daisy's tongue swelled too large for her mouth, making her resemble a pug with a hanging tongue. She gasped, and died.

2

"No." I tilted her head back and attempted to perform CPR with lips and hands that were quickly becoming covered with the same mysterious rash.

Angela, now free of the cream, attempted to wipe at my face. I shrugged her off. "I'm trying to save someone."

"But what if you leave that on for too long and die … like she did?"

Good point. "Someone take over while I clean my face."

Norma dropped to her knees and took my place. Sirens wailed in the distance, soon speeding up the driveway, followed by my detective boyfriend, Matthew Steele.

"Who called Matt?" I turned and glared at Mom, whose face was amazingly clear.

She shrugged. "He would only be upset if we didn't call."

I sighed and waited for the storm. I'd just gotten the last of the poisonous mask, after all, what else could be causing this type of reaction, off my face when Matt stormed into the house. He took one look at me, and froze.

Paramedics rushed in behind him and took Norma's place at Daisy's side. Their eyes widened as they glanced around the room. "What kind of party is this?" One of them asked.

"Beauty products." Angela covered her face with her hands and sobbed, collapsing into a chair. "I killed that poor woman."

"No, you didn't." Mom put an arm around her. "That devil mask did the deed."

By the way my skin burned, she wasn't too far off the mark. I'd have to die to feel better.

"I have questions." Matt held up a finger. "In a minute. No one leaves. No one speaks to each other."

As if he could keep a room full of women from talking. There was a whole lot being said by glances and facial expressions, and if I was reading the signs correctly, the mass majority didn't seem too upset that little Daisy had perished.

I sat on my hands to keep from scratching my face, also wanting to relieve the itching in the tips of my fingers that I'd used to scoop the cream from the container. Merciful heavens, it was agony.

The paramedics announced Daisy dead on arrival and stepped aside for a man wearing a vest stating he was the medical examiner. That meant we were going to be there for a long time, while he examined the body, and the paramedics tended to the rest of us.

Matt handed the container of pink poison to a waiting police officer, then turned to me. He scratched his chin. "Well, uh, it doesn't look like foul play, but do you know whether anyone here had anything against ..." he glanced at his notes, "Daisy Warner?"

"Everyone seems to get along just fine." In fact, they all seemed like the best of friends. If not for the lack of tears, I'd believe it. Were Angela and I the only ones who seemed saddened by Daisy's demise?

I had expected some competition among them, regarding their chosen profession, but that seemed absent, too. Something was up among the girls, and if I discovered Daisy had not died by an innocent allergic reaction, I'd be digging around to find out what secrets they hid. "Except, I don't think they're bosom buddies."

"Yeah, I noticed the lack of sorrow, too. Let me see one of your hands."

I pulled it out from under me. "Don't touch the rash. I don't know if it's contagious."

"It looks just like the time I sat in poison ivy as a kid." He turned my hand over. "Would it work this fast?"

"Maybe. I know Angela and I are both sensitive to the plant." Poison Ivy? Could it actually kill someone? "It doesn't affect Mom at all." I eyed her unblemished skin. "If what you're thinking is true, Matt, that means Daisy was murdered."

He put a finger over my lips. "Keep this between us for now, okay?

My heart stuttered, and I nodded. Why did these things keep happening to me?

A paramedic pushed between Matt and me and rubbed a cool ointment on my skin that brought immediate relief. I closed my eyes and sighed with pleasure.

Matt laughed. "You make that same sound when I kiss you."

"This feels almost as nice."

He patted the top of my head. "I'll drive you home. Wait while I question the others."

I strained my ears trying to hear his conversation with each woman. I couldn't make out a single word when he questioned Angela, her cries covered every other sound, and Mom eventually told him to move on and that he could question her tomorrow.

"That's fine, but we'll need to take her entire makeup kit for analysis." He nodded for someone to remove the kit, causing Angela to wail louder.

"I'll never have enough money for a place of my own!" She reached for the kit, glanced at the gurney wheeling

Daisy's body away, and wailed louder. Her arms fell to her sides.

I wanted to feel sorry for her, I really did, but considering I was paying a lot of money to renovate my attic into an apartment for her, she really shouldn't consider moving any time soon. "Can we go home now?"

"I still have a bit to do. Go ahead and go with your Mom and sister. I'll stop by later." Matt started to kiss me, then pulled back. "I like a woman with full lips, but yours are a bit much." He gave me a quick peck.

"You're hilarious." Really? My lips were swollen? Come to think of it, my throat felt bit tight. I waved a paramedic over. "I might need an epi pen or something."

He gave me a shot of something, then made the rounds again. "My suggestion is that all of you go to the hospital for overnight surveillance, especially since a woman died."

Good idea. I rushed to my car, motioning for Mom and Angela to follow and soon sat in the hospital Emergency Room. A doctor checked us over, said we didn't need to spend the night. If we hadn't died by now, we most likely wouldn't.

Wonderful. Nothing sounded better to me than going home.

Mom elected to drive, since the ride to the hospital had tortured my hands. I didn't argue. For once, I'd let her nurse me.

At home, we walked in the door to be greeted by two teenagers who took one look and burst into laughter. Mom giggled right along with them before telling them it wasn't nice to laugh at someone else's misfortune. I could still hear her chuckling on her way to the kitchen.

Leaving her to come up with supper on her own, I headed to the bathroom that connected my bedroom with my office. Since I had yet to get a good look at myself since Angela's disastrous beauty session, I made a beeline for the mirror.

My face was covered with blisters, not to mention the high sheen the ointment the paramedic spread on me made me look as if I was covered in shellac. My lips looked as if ten bees had stung them or a plastic surgeon injected too much collagen. Luckily, my eyes were unaffected, but I looked a mess.

"Did Mom's stuff do that to you?" Cherokee leaned in the doorway.

"Yes." I almost told her about the woman who had died, but held my tongue. My niece and nephew had been subjected to enough murder and mayhem the last year. This one was almost over. I'd try to spare them more torture. "Weird, huh?"

She shrugged. "I heard Mom saying that everyone except Grandma broke out. That's the weird part."

Which made me think even more that someone had laced the cream with poison ivy. A high concentration of it, too. But, why? Had they known Daisy was severely allergic? Or was it merely a prank gone too far?

"It is very strange." I washed my hands, dabbing the water from them rather than rubbing. If it was poison ivy, then breaking the blisters would only cause it to spread. The drying and cracking of the face mask had broken enough of them.

"Catch!" Dakota tossed a bottle of pink calamine lotion at me. "Grandma told me to give this to you."

"Thanks." So, it was a shiny face or a pink powdery one. Some choice. It was a very good thing I didn't have to go anywhere for a few days. "Ask her why she didn't buy the clear calamine."

"She said she already had bottles of this from … I can't remember." He dashed away to do whatever fifteen year old boys do.

His more mature seventeen year old sister rolled her eyes as only girls can do. "I wouldn't want to run around looking like cotton candy, but you can do what you want." She flounced off.

I stared at the bottle. If Mom couldn't remember where she got it, there was no telling how old it was. I fished my cell phone out of my pocket and texted Matt to bring a couple bottles of the clear stuff.

He responded that he would and to save him a plate at supper. I smiled and headed to the kitchen. The aroma of baking chicken filled the space.

"What can I help you with? Matt is coming over." I pulled up a chair to the island. There were a couple of casseroles in the freezer that only needed to be warmed through. I tended to cook when I was nervous or stuck in writer's block. Something my family was very grateful for.

"I don't want you touching anything with those hands. Who knows what kind of disease you all contracted." Mom shook a wooden spoon at me. "They should have quarantined all of you."

"You were there to." I grabbed a cherry tomato from a bowl.

"They had no reason to keep me. Robert will be here, too, so we'll have to eat in the dining room instead of the kitchen."

I still didn't know what to make of Mom's boyfriend, Robert Smithfield, the banker of Oak Meadows. Whenever the man came over, he said little and grinned a lot. That type of behavior didn't seem natural to me.

When the doorbell rang, I raced the teenagers to answer it, and threw myself into Matt's arms, kissing his cheek, then grabbing the paper bag out of his hands. "The stuff the paramedic used has worn off."

When you're finished doctoring yourself, meet me in the

living room. I have some news."

His grave look sent a rivulet of ice through my veins. I motioned my head to tell the kids to leave the room. "Tell me now."

He led me by the elbow into the living room. "Daisy had a note in her purse telling her that she had been warned that if she opened her mouth she would regret it."

"You think she was purposely put into contact with something that killed her?"

"Her medical records say she's deathly allergic to poison ivy." He put his hands on my shoulders. "The facial cream was full of it. It seems my dear, that you're going to be itching for a while."

I nibbled the inside of my bottom lip. Daisy had been murdered. I'd been thrust right back into a mystery.

3

"Angela!" I pulled free of Matt and yelled up the stairs. "Angela!"

"I'm coming." She paused at the top of the stairs, saw Matt, and descended like her version of a queen, all tottering high heels and tight dress. The effect she tried to portray was sorely distorted by her red, blotchy face. "Didn't Mom teach you not to screech like a barn owl? Hello, Matthew."

"Hey." The corners of his mouth twitched. "May we speak with you in the living room?"

"Is this on official police business?"

"Yes." He motioned his head toward the sofa.

She sighed and preceded us into the room. Sitting primly on the edge of the sofa, she crossed her ankles. Her eyes widened as Matt explained how Daisy died.

"Was your cream ever left unattended at this party of yours?" Matt pulled out a notepad.

"No." Tears welled in her eyes again. "I knew I killed her!"

I needed to teach my older sister never to blurt anything out to a police officer, Matt or not. "Yes, you did. After the ladies washed off their makeup, everyone crowded into the kitchen for snacks."

Matt gave me a quick glance. "Everyone?"

"I didn't pay that close of attention. I was starving." At

least we could narrow our suspects down to those attending the party. "Are prostitutes competitive?"

"Stay out of this one, Stormi." Matt gave me "the look".

I really didn't know why he bothered. Anyone who knew me would know jumping into a new mystery had become an addiction to me. Maybe there was a Gum Shoe Anonymous group I could join.

Angela wiped her tears away with the back of her hand. "Oh, stop it, Matthew. The only way to keep Stormi from being nosy is to lock her up."

"Well, I am the head of the Neighborhood Watch. It's my job to be nosy." I crossed my arms.

"Norma doesn't live in the same neighborhood as you," Matt pointed out. "There is no reason for you to get involved."

The rash on my face begged to differ. Normally, I wasn't one to exact revenge, but the small amount of vanity I possessed ached for justice. Add in the fact that I'd found the plot for my next book, and there was no way I could *stay out of things* as Matt so eloquently put it. My fans were anxiously awaiting the next "true crime" romantic mystery. Thankfully, this latest didn't seem like an overzealous fan wanting their moment of fame.

"Norma is my friend. Is she a suspect?" I asked.

"Everyone is a suspect," Matt said.

"I'm too pretty to go to jail." Angela covered her face and wailed.

I rolled my eyes and met Matt's amused glance. My sister definitely had a flair for the dramatic.

"Coffee?" Mom, her face still as clear of blotches as at the party, carried in a tray with cups, cakes, and a carafe. "I couldn't help but overhear. Let me say that I am thrilled not to be allergic to poison ivy."

Matt jumped up to take the tray from her. "That's a

miracle considering the high concentration in that cream."

"My complexion is flawless," she said. "I saw no reason to slather on the stuff an inch thick."

I hadn't either, but it hadn't saved me.

"This is going to be so bad for my business," Angela said. "No one will ever buy from me."

"It wasn't your fault." Mom handed out the cups and started pouring the coffee. "Once Matthew clears everything up, you'll be back in business. Stop crying."

"You're heartless." Angela dashed upstairs, taking her coffee with her.

I eyed the brown drops of liquid on my hardwood floors and grabbed a napkin from the tray. I wiped the spill and halfway listened while Mom and Matt discussed the party. For the life of me, I couldn't see a reason for one of the other gals to murder little Daisy. Their camaraderie must have been a façade for something deeper.

Tossing the soiled napkin back on the tray, I picked up my mug and added cream, watching the lighter colored circles swirl as I stirred. How long would it have taken for someone to add poison ivy and mix into the container? How did one even get liquid poison ivy? So many questions. I itched, literally, to sit in front of my laptop and do some research.

Without researching, I suppose someone could blend up the leaves into a pulp, squeeze out the liquid, and then add to a cream base. It could work, but it seemed like an awful lot of trouble to go to when simple poison or a gun would be easier. Still, it *was* a creative method of murder. I needed to find a way to "get in" with Norma's friends.

"I can see the wheels turning in your head, Stormi." Matt set his cup back on the tray. "Stop it."

"I can't stop thinking. It's impossible."

"Just tell him you're working on your book plot," Mom said. "That's what you always tell me when you go off into your own private world.”

“I’m sitting right here, Ann.” Matt shook his head. “Stormi doesn’t have a habit of zoning out when she’s with me.”

True, the man had a way of keeping my full attention. God broke the mold when he made Matthew Steele. My heart skipped a beat every time I looked at him.

“Stop staring at Matthew like you want to eat him.” Mom scowled. “Or at least wait until I leave the room.”

“I’ve seen the way you look at Robert.” I grinned.

‘I’m a widowed woman. I can stare hungrily if I want to.” Mom chuckled. “I’ll leave you two alone. I need to look over my baking list for tomorrow anyway.”

Ever since I helped Mom open her own baking business, she’d been busier than a one-armed paper hanger, and happier than a child at Christmas. Yes, I tended to think in clichés, despite being an author who knew it was a no-no to write them.

I moved and sat in Matt’s lap. “Wanna make out?”

He eyed my skin and swollen lips. “Uh—”

“It isn’t contagious.” I slapped his shoulder.

He laughed and pinned my arms behind me then nuzzled my neck, sending me into fits of screams which quickly turned to another sound altogether when he nibbled my earlobe. Who wanted to kiss? Kissing was overrated.

“Gross.” My nephew, Dakota, ducked into the room, grabbed his jacket from the back of the sofa, and darted back out.

I giggled, burying my face in Matt’s neck. “My family needs their own place.”

“That might be too dangerous for us.” He smiled. “I think we need the chaperonage.”

True. The man did tend to make me lose my sense. I sighed and laid my head on his chest. His heart raced, making me smile again to know I affected him as strongly as he did me.

His arms tightened around me. "You're going to stick your nose into Daisy's death, aren't you?"

What a way to spoil the mood. "I'm only going to question Norma to see whether she knows if any of the other women have a grudge against Daisy. That's all."

"I wish I believed that."

"I have no desire to go looking for trouble. A few questions are harmless."

"You may not go looking for it, but trouble follows you like a swarm of mosquitos in a swamp."

"Yuck."

He laughed, his chest rumbling against my cheek. "The police department doesn't really have the manpower to assign you a guard every time you go nosing around."

"What about Koontz?" I'd grown quite fond of the large black man during my last mystery episode.

"He's on assignment."

"Then that leaves you to protect me." Not that I expected to need protection. Death by poison ivy, while it had looked like a horrible way to die, didn't seem to be particularly vicious. As long as I didn't eat, drink, or put on anything not prepared by my own hands, I should be all right.

Cherokee, my niece, cleared her throat in the doorway. I glanced up to see a boy I didn't recognize. That girl changed boyfriends as often as her mother did shoes. "Blake and I would like to watch TV."

"Go ahead," I said.

"We can't while the two of you are … doing that."

"We aren't doing anything."

"Whatever. We'll go to my room."

I jumped off Matt's lap. "Oh, no, you won't. We'll move to the front porch." I grabbed an afghan off the back of the chair. December nights grew cold.

"That's okay," Matt said, planting a kiss on the top of my head. "I need to get home. There are some phone calls I need to make."

Oh, I hoped they had to do with the case and that his sister, Maryann, was home to eavesdrop. That girl could sneak up on her brother like nobody's business. Since she had accepted the job as my part time literary assistant, she'd be over after she finished teaching school the next day. I couldn't wait to fill her in on all that was happening.

I cupped Matt's cheek. "See you tomorrow."

He kissed my palm. "Tomorrow. Love you."

I sighed and walked him to the door, wanting more than a quick "love you". I wanted the three words "I love you" spoken in a moment of great tenderness. I should be content that a confirmed bachelor got as close to saying those words as Matt did, but I wasn't. Maybe I should say the words first. But what if he didn't respond in kind?

My bed called. It had been a long day.

Steps dragging, I carried the coffee tray into the kitchen and set it by the sink. I'd clean it in the morning. As I climbed the stairs to my room, I texted Norma. "Are you free for coffee in the morning?" I didn't need to tell her where. It was unspoken that we would meet where her son worked … Delicious Aroma. The new owners didn't have much of an imagination as far as names went, but the coffee couldn't be beat.

"Sure," she responded. "I'll bring notes."

I had the best friends. Grinning, I headed for the shower. My circle of crime solving friends now numbered four: Me, Matt's sister, Mom, and Norma. If Matt kept too tight of a rein on me, one of the others stepped in to gather information.

It got a bit dangerous at times, such as the crazy neighbor I once had who killed everyone who had been mean to her mentally challenged son, or the crazed fan who stalked me via email trying to threaten me into writing my next book quicker. When I wrote a parody making fun of the stalker, the woman, the town's librarian, kidnapped me and forced me to write at gunpoint.

No one could say my life was boring. I turned on the shower and shed my clothes, then eyed the container of ointment Mom had given me earlier for my rash. I knew there wasn't anything harmful in it, since I'd applied it a few hours earlier, but I still felt a moment of trepidation. I laughed it off and stepped into the shower.

The hot water ran over my head and shoulders, washing away the day's stress. I closed my eyes and let the day's events run through my mind. Five women, all excited about beauty products, until one ends up dead. Who hated Daisy enough to go to so much trouble to kill her?

I pictured the women's stricken expressions when Daisy fell to the floor in agony. One of them was a very good actress. I intended to find out which one.

4

I welcomed Norma the next morning with a smile and a cup of coffee at Delicious Aroma. As was customary, Sarah Thompson typed away on her laptop in the corner. Thankfully, she was so busy, she had yet to notice me.

"What a pickle." Norma said, breathing deeply above her coffee, the aroma tantalizingly wonderful.

"Who says that anymore?" I sipped my blended mocha drink. "I hope you don't put clichés like that in your writing."

"No worries." She grinned. "I think the fan fiction I write of your stories would meet with your approval. Except for the added smut, of course."

"Of course." While my books weren't what one would call prudish, I didn't think erotic elements were necessary to tell a good story. "I'm assuming the pickle you're talking about is Daisy's death?"

She nodded."It has to be someone at the party."

"Agreed. Who had a grievance with her?"

"No one. Daisy was as sweet as her name." Norma shook her head. "Even when I did their line of work, I never heard anyone say anything bad about her. But ... there were rumors."

"Of?"

She pulled a small notepad out of her gigantic Fuschia

pink shoulder bag. "If this gets into the hands of the wrong person, we're dead. I hope you realize how dangerous this is."

I definitely knew danger. I'd come face-to-face with it twice now. Still, I was in no hurry to face it again. "Maybe this isn't the place to discuss this. Let's head across the street to my mother's shop."

"Perfect. I could use some sweets." Norma shoved her pad back in her purse and headed out the door and across the street as if Mom would run out of cupcakes before Norma arrived.

Mom's shop was empty except for her and her hired help, Greta, a former police officer Mom enlisted to help with our last gumshoeing escapade. Mom glanced up from where she designed frosting roses on top of a wedding cake. "Stormi, Norma, what brings you two over here this early?"

"We need a private place to discuss Norma's notes." I used my finger to scoop up a bit of misplaced icing from the counter top. "Norma is hoping for a cupcake."

"Take anything from the ready-mades," Mom said.

Norma chose a red velvet with cream cheese frosting. "You don't mind if we sit in the customer area, do you?"

"Not as long as you talk loud enough for me and Greta to hear."

"Maybe we should bring a couple of chairs in here," I suggested. We wouldn't want to be overheard by any customers.

"Good idea." Norma tottered on her four inch heels and dragged one of the bistro style chairs from the front of the shop to the back.

I perched on one of the work stools. Unless I was on a date with Matt, I chose not to wear tight dresses and heels. A girl couldn't run in them, and I'd had a few times I needed to put on the speed. No, I'd stick to jeans, a pretty blouse, and nice gym shoes.

"Okay, now tell me your news." I leaned forward, balancing my elbows on my knees.

"Remember, this is only a rumor." Norma crossed her long shapely legs. "Word on the street is that Daisy saw something she shouldn't."

"You'll have to give me more than that."

"I may not walk the streets in a business capacity any longer," Norma said. "But when I do wander the streets in order to see old friends, people still act as if I belong there." She grinned. "A man actually tried to proposition me last night."

It might have something to do with the way she dressed, but I decided the wisest course of action was to keep my mouth shut. "What did she see?"

Norma lowered her voice. "A gang murder."

Mom gasped, Greta glanced at the window, and I straightened. I didn't want anything to do with anything that had to do with gangs. This was one mystery I didn't want to solve. "You need to stop snooping around, Norma. These aren't people you want to mess with."

"She's right," Greta said. "Gangs don't care if you're a man or woman. If you get in their way—"

Norma glanced at each of us. "I thought it would be a great new mystery story for Stormi to write about."

"No, way. For once, I'm listening to Matt and letting the police handle this one."

Norma's face fell. "The people I know won't talk to the police, but they will talk to prostitutes." She cast a sharp gaze on me. "It wouldn't take much to turn you into a street walker. You could blend right in."

I wasn't sure whether I should feel insulted or pleased. "No, this is one I'm going to stay out of."

"I'm glad you've finally come to your senses." Mom

pulled a sheet cake from the oven.

"Don't act like you're innocent in all this." I hopped off the stool. "You're the one who came up with a name for our nosiness."

She glared at me. "The Hickory Hellos are a welcoming committee."

"I want to join," Norma said. "Then, we could snoop under the banner of the committee, expanding to my neighborhood."

"You don't live on Hickory." Mom set the pan on a cooling rack.

"Fine." Norma stood and tugged her short dress to the middle of her thighs. "I'll have to find out what happened to Daisy on my own. I thought you women cared, but I was mistaken. You only care if it directly affects you." She narrowed her eyes at me. "I doubt anyone will ever buy any of your sister's products." With her head held high, she sailed out the door.

I hated disappointing her, but having dealt with a psycho neighbor and a mentally disturbed librarian within the course of a year, left me with little desire to move on to bigger dangers. Not to mention the fact that Matt would absolutely kill me.

"You made the right decision," Greta said. "If she's as good a friend as you say she is, she'll get over it and see the wisdom in your refusal."

I hoped so. I swiped a piece of chocolate cake left over from something Mom had created, and headed home to work on my writing. My second full length mystery was loosely based on Daisy's death, and even though I had no desire to go asking questions of gang members, it would be a nice addition to the story.

Back at home, I disengaged the alarm system installed during the last threat against me, and headed straight to my office. I booted up my computer and turned to stare out the window at my tranquil neighborhood of well-manicured lawns. Except for mine. Ever since Rusty Henley, after finding out his mother was a murderer, had disappeared, getting my lawn mowed and weeded had taken a back seat to other obligations. Still, unless I wanted a nasty letter from the Home Owner's Association, I'd have to hire another gardener. I missed the kind, simple-minded, Peeping Tom Rusty.

The first thing I did once my computer came on was to check my emails, grateful that I no longer had to worry about a stalker threatening me to rush writing my next book. My agent wasn't nagging me about a deadline yet, either. I promised her two books a year, and if I wasn't off trying to catch murderers, could probably produce three a year. There was no sense in rushing a good thing, though, right?

Two hours and three thousand words later, I decided it was time to call Norma and try to patch our friendship. After four rings, her voice mail picked up. I left a message for her to call me, then headed to the kitchen for a sandwich.

I leaned against the counter as I ate and watched Sadie dash around the backyard, nose to the ground, bent on a mission. I'd been so busy lately, I'd forsaken our nightly walks. The evenings were chilly, but wouldn't bother the Irish Wolfhound. I promised myself I would take her for a walk after supper.

I tried calling Norma again and left another message. Maybe I should drive to her house and apologize in person. I grabbed my car keys from the foyer table, set the alarm, and dashed through the chilly day to my Mercedes. Until Mom's basement apartment was completed, I had no room to park in the garage and had to leave my "baby" outside.

As in most cities, you had a wide range of neighborhoods. I had the pleasure of living in upper middle class, Norma in lower. I pulled into her driveway and waved at the familiar group of youth standing on the street corner.

"She ain't home." Jamal, Norma's neighbor, strode toward me in that loose-legged, hitched stroll that teenage boys seemed to be the only ones to master. "She's working Melrose."

"Working?" I frowned. "I thought she quit … that job."

He shrugged. "Guess she likes it after all." Keeping his posture belligerent, he lowered his voice. "You stick out like a sore thumb with that white skin and red hair. I hope you ain't coming around to ask questions. My homies won't like it. Word on the street is that you like to poke your nose where it don't belong."

Word on the street? "People are talking about me?" A shard of ice stabbed my gut.

He nodded. "Ever since Daisy died, folks are wanting to know iffen you're going to get involved. I advise against it."

"There isn't anything to get involved in, Jamal. Daisy died because she was allergic to poison ivy."

"Who put the poison in that face cream?" He poked me in the chest. "Look. I like you, but I'm saying you need to stay away from this side of town." He turned and shuffled back to his homies.

His advice sounded close to being a threat. Why did everyone automatically assume I was going to be nosy? I was starting to get a complex.

I got back in my car and headed to Melrose Street. I doubted that Norma was actually turning tricks again, but just pretending to could get her killed. Why was she so bent on finding the killer of a girl she had barely known?

Afraid to park my car and leave it unattended, I slowly cruised the street. When I finally spotted Norma, I honked my horn and pulled alongside her. Another girl started to approach, saw me behind the wheel and stalked off, saying she didn't swing that way. I shrugged. "Norma."

She leaned in the window. "What are you doing here? You're going to blow my cover."

"Get in the car. This is too dangerous." I hit the button to unlock the door.

She sighed and slid in. "Did you change your mind?"

"No." I pulled away from the curb. "I did come to apologize though. Jamal told me where to find you."

"Stay away from him, Stormi."

We pulled into her driveway. I stayed in the car and glanced toward the group of boys. "He warned me about getting involved, so I'm now warning you."

Her hands shook as she lit a cigarette. I normally didn't allow people to smoke in my car, but understood her nervousness. I rolled the window down a few inches.

She took a puff. "If they're warning you, they already think you're involved. I'd find someplace to hide out for a while."

Although I wasn't a smoker, I was tempted to take a drag. I clutched my shaky hands around the steering wheel. "What about you?"

She shrugged. "I'm one of them."

"So was Daisy."

Without looking at me, she said, "That's why I need your help before something to happens to me."

5

Norma knew just what to say to get me to agree to help her. At least I drove home and called Matt before doing anything stupid, unless you count my response to Norma's plea as not the brightest thing I've ever done.

He sat at my kitchen table, hands clenched on the table in front of him. "You told her what?"

"She pleaded with me to help her."

"You aren't in law enforcement. She should have gone to the police." He ran his hands through his wheat-colored hair, making it stand on end like stalks of golden fields. "When are you going to learn?"

It was a very good thing that I left out Jamal's warning. "I'm getting quite good at solving mysteries."

"Out of sheer luck!" He bolted to his feet and planted his hands, palm down, on the table with enough force to rattle the spoons in our coffee mugs. "You've faced down the barrel of a gun both times."

"Both times, my wit and ingenuity have gotten me out alive."

He shook his head. "All you've done in the past is put your nose where it didn't belong and get lucky. Think about it, Stormi. You haven't solved these crimes. You've been a victim both times, and the police has rescued you."

I straightened in my chair. "Only because I discovered

enough evidence to make the guilty person nervous." There was no way he could convince me that I didn't have a hand in the capture of two seriously mentally-ill killers. If I didn't, then what was I thinking? Why write my romantic mysteries from the point-of-view of first person … me?

"Why won't you listen to me?" He moved around the table, took my hands in his, and pulled me to my feet. "Every time you put yourself in harm's way, I die a little. Don't you care?"

"Of course, I do." Tears welled in my eyes. "But if you know me, then you know I can't turn away someone who needs me."

"Let *me* help Norma."

I stared into his chocolate-colored eyes, ready to tell him everything Jamal had said.

"Aunt Stormi." Cherokee leaned in the doorway. "Sorry to break up the lovefest, but I can't find my backpack and I'm headed to Megans to do homework."

I sighed and pulled away. "Check the living room. The last time you lost it, it fell behind the sofa." The moment for true confessions had passed. If I told Matt about Jamal, and the boy was questioned by the police, it could increase the danger to myself and Norma, thus putting my family in danger. How could an innocent ladies party have turned into this?

"Thanks." She ducked back out of sight.

"You're keeping something from me," Matt said. "It's the first month of a new year. Can't we try and start it off on the right foot? The beginning of a year without secrets?"

The month of December had flown by, Angela wailed over lost Christmas sales, and I'd done nothing to help her. What kind of a sister was I?

Oh, how I wanted to. I gazed into his eyes again, a big mistake, since it always made me lose my resolve, and start talking. I told him about Norma's rumors, Jamal's threat, everything, even repeating what I had said before.

His face reddened to the point I thought his head might explode. "Why weren't you going to tell me?"

"I don't want you questioning Jamal. I don't want the gang to come to my house. There are teenagers living here." And my nephew Dakota wouldn't think twice about mouthing off if someone threatened us.

"I can't take another leave of absence to protect you." He inhaled sharply through his nose. "And, I can't keep asking Ryan to babysit you."

I didn't think Koontz would mind, especially since it seemed as if an attraction was growing between him and my sister, but I agreed. I was on my own on this one. The thought turned my blood to ice. "Maybe it's all smoke and mirrors. The threat might mean nothing. I'll be discreet."

"Once again, I've lost the argument." Matt dug his car keys from his pocket. "I've got things to do." He planted a quick kiss on my lips and left.

I sagged onto my seat. What had I ever done to deserve such a man? Once, he'd had enough of worrying about me, and I'd broken off our relationship. To no avail. He had refused to take no for an answer. How long until he was the one who called it quits?

I needed to make friends with Jamal and his "homies". One glance at the clock showed it was pizza time. I ordered three large pizzas. When they arrived, I left a note on the refrigerator that supper was inside, then took one of the pizzas outside to my car. I texted Norma that I was coming and drove to her place.

As with every other time I'd been there, Jamal and his friends were on the street corner. Didn't they have anything else to do? Didn't the January weather bother them?

I grabbed the pizza and strolled through light snowflakes

in their direction. "You boys hungry?"

"What are you doing here?" Jamal took the box and handed it to one of the other guys. "Don't you listen to reason?"

"If you asked my boyfriend, he would tell you no."

"That cop?"

I nodded.

"He know you're here?"

"Should he?" I wrapped my arms around my middle in an attempt to keep warm. These boys seemed to be around Dakota's age. Maybe Mom was wrong about food being the best way to break into a teenage boy's world.

"You scared?" Jamal sneered.

"Nope." I turned, my insides skittering like ants, and headed for Norma's front door. "Just spending time with a friend and thought you boys would like the leftover pizza."

"The pizza is still warm," he called out.

My legs were trembling by the time I rang Norma's doorbell. She opened it and yanked me inside. "You are the craziest person I've ever met. Those boys are dangerous."

"They aren't so bad." Ivy, one of the women from the party, crossed her long dark legs. "The pizza was a nice touch."

I glanced around the living room, noting Ivy, Ginger, Lacey, and Sissy all sipping on glasses of wine. "You have company. I'll go."

"Stay." Norma waved me toward an empty seat. "It's only our monthly meeting."

"It's her attempt at getting us to clean up our lives," Lacey said. "We come for the food and wine."

Norma shrugged. "At least they're honest. Wine?"

I shook my head. Now what? I couldn't very well talk to Norma about my conversation with Matt with virtual strangers hanging on every word. Maybe the meeting wouldn't last long. After all, night time was their best working hours, right? And maybe I was making a totally rash, clichéd assumption.

I sat back and listened as Norma spoke of all the ways that leaving the oldest profession in the world behind her had benefited her. From the bored looks on her friends' faces, they'd heard it all before. I felt sorry for my friend. She tried so hard. But, since I didn't have anything better to say, I kept my mouth shut.

My cell phone buzzed. It was Matt asking where I was. He had gone back to my house, only to find out I was gone. I couldn't very well tell him where I was, so I ignored the text.

"Is that from your handsome cop boyfriend?" Ivy grinned, her teeth startling against her ebony skin. "Maybe you should invite him over to liven up this meeting."

"Thanks a lot, Ivy." Norma frowned. "I'm being serious here and all you can think about is a man. A taken one at that."

"Honey, most of the men who buy my time are taken." Ivy set her empty glass on the coffee table. "I appreciate what you're trying to do here, but my man likes the money I bring in. I don't see that changing anytime soon, for me or my sisters-in-crime."

"Our Johns aren't as understanding as yours was," Lacey said. "We even hint at leaving and we get punched."

"They can't make you stay." Tears welled in Norma's eyes. "Do you know what the lifespan for a prostitute is?"

"That's why I plan on grabbing everything I can now," Sissy said. "While I'm a hot commodity."

"Y'all are hopeless." Norma grabbed a napkin and wiped her eyes. "I worry about you, that's all."

"You need to stop coming down to Melrose, too." Ivy stood. "Some of the other girls are complaining about you infringing on their turf. If you want to see us, keep having the meetings, otherwise, it's time we parted ways."

"I'll keep having the meetings. I won't give up." Norma headed to the door to let them out. Once they were gone, she plopped down next to me. "I know you're here for a reason. Spill it."

I told her of Matt's concerns about me getting involved. "Not to mention the fact that I haven't the slightest idea where to start asking questions about Daisy."

"I found out a bit tonight." Norma refilled her wine glass. "Turns out our little flower might not have been as sweet as she seemed. She'd been threatening some people, bad people, about something she knew. None of the girls knew what that might be. As usual, it's just rumor, but it might be our motive."

My cell phone buzzed again. I told Matt I was out to dinner with Norma. "Let's go grab a burger. I don't want to lie to Matt again."

"Let's go to Leroy's. They don't act like they want to throw me out every time I walk though the door." Norma grabbed her purse and followed me out to my car. "You don't mind if we bring something back for Tyler, do you? He's always hungry after working at the coffee shop."

"Of course not. You must be very proud of him." I eyed Jamal and his friends. "He kept away from that life."

"It wasn't easy. Him and Jamal grew up together. They're friends, but not close anymore. If we didn't still live in the neighborhood, I'd fear for his safety when they met."

"Is Jamal that bad?"

"He can be." Norma clicked her seatbelt across her. "Then, at other times, he's the sweetest guy. That boy is a product of his environment. I pray every day that he finds a way out. Sissy is his sister."

"Really?" I glanced at him again. "They don't look anything alike."

"Different daddy, most likely."

I backed the car from the driveway and kept backing up until I pulled alongside Jamal. "Hand me the empty box off the sidewalk, would you? Have a little respect for where you live."

He laughed and handed me the box. "Why do you care? You drive up here with your charity pizza and fancy car."

Norma leaned across me. "Don't sass! This is my friend. She's welcome here any time she wants. You be nice, or I'll tell your mama."

"Whatever." He turned away.

I pulled away from the curb after tossing the box in the back seat. "His mama?"

"That's the only thing that will get to him. That boy loves his mama. She works two jobs just to keep a roof over their heads while he does nothing but cause trouble. It's a shame. You'll meet her soon. She's a waitress at Leroy's."

"Does she know Daisy?"

"I doubt it Shaunda Brown is an upstanding, church going woman. She barely talks to me, and only when she has to."

I pulled into the parking lot of Leroy's Bar and Grill, my stomach rumbling from the smell of the pizza box on my back seat. I wasn't sure whether meeting Shaunda would help solve the mystery surrounding Daisy's death or not, but it wouldn't hurt to get to know the mother of the boy I was trying to befriend.

Make friends with the mother and maybe the son wouldn't kill me.

6

Not wanting Matt to worry anymore, I texted to let him know where we were eating and followed a young girl to a table in a darkened corner. Norma had requested a table in Shaunda's area and the hostess was happy to oblige.

Before our waitress approached our table, Matt strolled through the door, glanced around the room, then made a beeline to our table. He sat between Norma and I, fixing me with his stare. "What's the topic of conversation, ladies?"

"Girl talk." Norma smiled and leaned back in her chair. I wanted to tell her that feminine wiles wouldn't work on my detective boyfriend, but decided to sit back and enjoy the show.

"Is that so? It wouldn't be because Jamal Brown's mother works here, would it? Is that why you chose Leroy's?"

Norma's smile never faltered. Oh, she was good. She leaned forward, her already low dress slipping lower. "I come here for the food, detective."

I would never resort to such measures to throw a man off his train of thought, but couldn't help but enjoy Norma's efforts, which I was correct about not having any chance of success. A muscle ticked in Matt's jaw

He straightened as our waitress arrived.

"Hello, Norma." The woman's cold tone could have froze the Bahamas into a new ice age. "What can I get you and

36

your friends to drink?"

"I'll have tea," Matt said.

I ordered the same, with Norma ordering a glass of wine. How did she still walk on her high heels? This had to be her third glass of the night.

"Hey, Shaunda. We'll have our orders when you get back." Norma tilted her head at Matt. "What makes you suspect we're up to no good?"

"The pizza box in Stormi's back seat for one. She didn't have it there earlier. So, if you've already eaten, why come to a burger joint which serves enough food for several people off one order? Unless, you're here fishing for information." He unfolded his napkin and placed it on his lap.

I had hoped Matt might have forgotten I was there, but no such luck. He turned to me. "If you didn't eat the pizza, who did?"

"I gave it to Jamal."

Norma threw up her hands. "You don't have to tell your boyfriend everything you do in your life."

"We're working on no more secrets, aren't we, Stormi?" Matt's features looked set in granite.

I nodded. "I'm trying to befriend the boy, to, uh … show him another side of life." Not a lie, exactly. I would like nothing more than to pull him away from the gang life.

His stare deepened, but he didn't say anything until our drinks arrived and we all ordered bacon cheeseburgers. Once Shaunda had left, order pad in hand, he turned back to me. "Why are you really here? You can stop shaking your head, Norma. I see you out of the corner of my eye."

"We wanted to question Shaunda about some rumors we, or rather,Norma, heard about Daisy." I bent my head and concentrated on tearing the paper around my straw into a billion pieces.

"Girl, your mouth flaps at both ends." Norma threw her

straw at me.

"What rumors?" Matt, thankfully, transferred his attention back to Norma.

She proceeded to tell him what she had told me. "That's all I know. Speculation."

"Was someone killed that we don't know about?" I asked, lifting my head and sweeping my pile of paper into my hand. I dropped them in the basket that held artificial sugars.

"If it wasn't on the news, you don't need to know about it."

"Was it on the news?"

Matt's eyes narrowed. "Stop asking questions; of me or anyone else. You're treading on dangerous ground."

"I haven't asked anyone other than you any questions." Yet. "I told you I would be discreet and careful. I fully intend to do just that."

"Look, detective." Norma placed a well-manicured hand over his, removing it when he glared at it. "I'm doing all of the footwork on this one. Stormi is only my consultant."

"She's a romance writer, not a crime solver!" He rolled his head on his neck. "Let the police handle this."

"I don't have a lot of faith in the police, no offense." Norma sat back in her chair as Shaunda brought our burgers.

"Y'all ain't talking about my boy, are you?" She glanced at Norma. "He ain't bothering you?"

She waved off her concern. "Jamal is fine."

Shaunda nodded, glancing at me, then moved on to another table.

Matt lowered his voice. "Regardless of your personal feelings, the police are now involved. Further questioning on either of your parts will force me to arrest you for interfering with a murder investigation."

Oh, he was mad. He had threatened to arrest me before, but this was the first time I believed he might actually follow through on the threat. "I told you we weren't questioning anyone. I'm trying to get a kid off the streets so he doesn't end up like Daisy." I crossed my arms.

"Noble, but unwise considering the circumstances." Matt bit into his burger.

"I need to use the restroom." Hopefully, Matt won't have noticed Shaunda ducking into the ladies room. "Norma?"

"If you two aren't back in three minutes, I'm coming after you," Matt said. "If you try to sneak out, I'll follow you."

"Don't worry. We'll be back." I grabbed Norma's arm and dragged her after me.

Shaunda was leaning against the sink when we darted inside. "What's going on? Don't lie to me. I'm a mother. I can spot a lie through two inch mud."

"Did Jamal know Daisy?" I figured bluntness would work best.

"I try to keep him away from those sluts, but yes, they dated for a while last year." Shaunda sighed heavily. "Then, she broke if off real sudden like. Broke my boy's heart."

"Enough to kill her?"

"What are you accusing him of? Jamal might get in trouble now and then, but he never lays a hand on a girl. I taught him better than that." She leaned closer. "Or are you accusing me? I'll do anything for my boy, but I won't murder. Besides, how would I get my hands on poison ivy in the winter? Now, you two leave me and my boy alone." She reached for the door.

"I'm trying to befriend him to get him out of the gang."

"That's mighty white of you. Stay away from me and mine."

"Hey!" Few things made me madder than racism. I squeezed between her and the door. "If you want me to stay away because you're his mother, that's one thing, but you leave race and skin color out of it. I don't deserve that type of treatment."

Shaunda's face fell. "I'm sorry. I just worry about my boy. I didn't mean that. If you can get him away from that life, I will be forever grateful." She rushed out, leaving me and Norma alone.

Or so I thought, until the toilet flushed. Norma and I ducked into the handicap stall. I peered through the space between the door and the wall. Ginger, her dyed red hair piled high on her head, washed her hands at the sink. After drying them on paper towels, she turned.

"You can come out now. I know you're in there."

Like children caught stealing cookies, we shuffled from the stall. "You two are the worst snoops ever," she said. "If you're going to question someone in the bathroom, you should always check the other stalls first."

Someone knocked on the door. "Time's up," Matt called out.

Ginger laughed. "The cops are here. Time for two nosy Nelly's to go home. Watch your backs, ladies."

"What does she mean by that?" I hissed as she went out the door first.

Norma shrugged. "Seems like everyone is threatening us."

We followed Matt to our table.

"It looked like a regular party in there," he said. "You two must have been in heaven with the questions."

I shrugged. "Shaunda wanted us to clarify why we were interested in her son and Ginger just happened be in the stall. It was all very innocent."

"Sure it was." He finished his hamburger, threw a couple of twenty dollar bills on the table, then kissed me goodbye. "Drop Norma off and come straight home. I mean it."

"Yes, Dad." I grinned to take the bite off my words.

"That is why I don't settle down." Norma bit into a French-fry. "I don't want any man telling me what to do."

"It's more like Matt suggests and I might or might not do as he suggested." While feelings ran hot between us, no words of love had left either of our lips. I felt the words, but saying them seemed like a loss of freedom. Although I wrote romance books, I was completely messed up in that department.

"You might as well take me home." Norma slung her purse over her arm. "Just pull into the driveway. There's no reason for you to get out of the car."

I did as she suggested, then headed home. Sure enough, Matt was waiting in his car. I parked, and he followed me into the house.

"What did you find out in the restroom?" He asked as soon as I closed the front door.

"Ginger told us to watch our backs." I led the way into the kitchen. "And Shaunda told us that Jamal and Daisy were dating. She broke it off suddenly, leaving him devastated. That was it. A very unproductive interview."

"Not exactly. I didn't know that Jamal and Daisy had been an item." Matt sat at the table, smiling a welcome as Mom entered the kitchen.

"What's my daughter been up to now?"

"Her usual snooping."

"Greta and I already told her that a gang is nothing to mess with." Mom grabbed a glass from the cabinet. "Greta used to work undercover, posing as a landlord for a building one of the gangs lived in. Nasty business. The things that went on there would curdle your blood."

"That's gross, Mom." I tossed Matt a can of soda and grabbed a diet one for myself.

"I'm just saying that this is a mystery the Hickory Hellos need to stay out of."

"I agree," Matt said. "If you want to visit with Norma, have her come here."

"Doesn't it make more sense to snoop openly so the bad guys think we're on the up and up?" I took a big gulp of my drink. "If I stop going over there now, after being threatened, they'll think I actually had a reason to get threatened."

"That doesn't make any sense," Mom said.

"It does to me. I can't stop going to Norma's house all of a sudden. Not without a good reason." I opened the back door and let Sadie out. She dashed across the yard after a squirrel. "If you come up with a reason Jamal and his buddies will believe, then I'll stop going."

"Sure you will." Mom filled her glass with ice water. "I like a good mystery as well as the next person, but my shop keeps me busy. I can't be protecting you."

Matt choked on his drink.

Mom pounded him on the back. "I'm being serious, Matthew. I'm the one with common sense of the two of us. If not for me, there's no telling what mischief my daughter would get into." She sighed dramatically. "You'd think at her age that I could stop worrying as much. Not with Stormi."

"Very funny." I drained the rest of my soda and tossed my can in the recycle bin.

Something exploded out front, blowing out the front windows and setting off every car alarm in the neighborhood. Matt tackled me to the floor. Mom joined us, peering over the windowsill.

"Looks like you have a good reason not to visit Norma now," Mom said. "Your car is on fire."

I'd finally gotten something blown up.

7

"Stay here." Matt made a quick call to the precinct on his cell phone, another to the fire department, then dashed outside.

Of course Mom and I followed, earning us a frustrated glance from Matt. "It's a good thing no one was in the car," Mom said.

I inched as close as the heat would allow. "Somebody was."

Who in Hades would have been sitting in my car. I pulled out my cell phone and sent a group text to the members of my family stating we needed an emergency check-in. Seconds later, I'd gotten three texts confirming everyone was fine, but wanting to know what was going on. I didn't answer. They'd find out as soon as they arrived home.

Dakota beat the fire truck. He hopped off his skateboard, narrowly missing my feet. "Whoa. Exciting. Is that a body?"

"Move back." Matt waved his hand as the fire truck, followed by two squad cars, roared up the driveway.

The cheeseburger I had eaten jammed up my throat, threatening to burst free. The air was filled with the stench of burning pork. If only it had been a side of ham left in my car and not some unsuspecting stranger. By now, my neighbors were staring from their yards, reassuring me that the body wasn't one of theirs. I'm sure it didn't make some of them look more favorably on me as a neighbor, but that was their problem.

The fire department had the fire out in short order and the emergency technicians laid the body in a black bag and zipped it shut. Matt spoke with them for a few minutes, then joined us by the porch.

"It will take a few days before we have a positive ID," he said. "If I can tell you who it is, I will. Otherwise, you'll have to wait until the news like everyone else."

The three local channel television station reporters rushed toward the house like piranhas. I skirted past Mom and dashed into the house. Their shouted questions squeezed through even the miniscule cracks in the house.

"Miss Nelson! Do you know who the body in the car is?"

"Can you give us a quick comment?"

Was my mother invisible? She loved the limelight. Why couldn't they leave me alone and pester her?

"Are you going to write another book based on today's happenings?"

They converged on the porch, peering through the curtains. I made a dash for the kitchen, stopping short and screaming at a face plastered against the kitchen window. Sadie barked and scratched at the glass, trying in vain to get to our unwanted visitor. I headed upstairs to the sanctuary of my office, leaving Matt and the other officers to deal with the reporters.

Of course the car blowing up would go in my next book. I buried my face in my hands. I loved that car. Still, it was only a material possession. My heart ached at the person who had endured the fiery death.

Another glance out the window showed my mother animatedly talking to the reporters and Matt behind them waving his arms in a vain attempt to get her to stop talking. My nerves rang like a church bell. What in heaven's name could she possibly be telling them?

I raced downstairs, whipped open the front door, grabbed her arm, and then dragged her inside, which started the reporters' questions all over again.

"Miss Nelson, are you the target of a gang?"

"Do you know who was in your car?"

"Can you tell us who the gang leader is?"

I slammed the door. "Mom, what did you tell them?"

"I believe in the papers printing only the truth. I told them you had received threats from possible gang members." She headed to the kitchen. "Nothing that won't be common knowledge soon enough."

"Especially after you opened your mouth. Didn't you see Matt trying to get you to be quiet?" I perched on the edge of a kitchen chair and stared at her.

"I thought he was waving away a bee." She started making coffee.

"You've increased the danger to every one of us." My shoulders slumped. I really hadn't wanted to get involved this time, yet trouble knocked on my door anyway. The last two crimes I'd been involved in were nowhere near the magnitude of this one. I had literally stumbled over the first body, and the second time a psycho email stalker had dogged my every step. Why do these things keep happening to me?

Matt burst through the back door and stopped to glare at Mom. "Didn't you see me?"

"She thought you were swatting at bees."

"What?" He frowned.

"Never mind. Tell me the damage." I rested my elbows on the table.

"She laid it out, in simple language, everything that has been happening to you and Norma. If the gang didn't think you were involved in their business before, they will now." He pulled out a chair and sat down. "The department will try to keep the papers from printing anything, but that hasn't worked very well in the past. What were you thinking, Ann?"

"I guess I got caught up in the moment. Call it my fifteen minutes of fame." She handed us mugs of coffee. She set down and sighed. "I messed up. I'm sorry. I only meant to say one little thing and then put in a plug for my business. I got carried away."

Matt scratched his eyebrow. "I'll have to find around the clock protection for all of you. The department is already stretched thin. You've put me in a tough spot, Ann, and possibly jeopardized the investigation."

"Mom, I think it's time you and the others head to the family cabin."

"What about you?"

"I'll stay. If I go, I take the problem with me." My hands trembled around the mug. I wished I'd had more time to befriend Jamal. It could make a big difference in what happens to me.

She shook her head. "No, I made the mess, I'll stay here to help clean it up."

The reporters started shouting again and we raced to the window. Angela and Cherokee sat cornered in her van, eyes wide, terror on their faces as they watched a tow truck take away what remained of my car.

"I'd better go rescue your sister." Matt squared his shoulders and left through the back door.

Five minutes later, Dakota included, came back in, drawing reporters to the back of the house. Mom closed the curtains over the windows.

"What happened?" Angela sagged into a chair.

I explained, the best I could, not leaving out Mom's rambling story to the press. Once I'd finished, I sat back down and tried to get my hands to still around my mug.

Angela bolted to her feet. "I have to take my children away from here."

"I want to stay." Dakota crossed his arms. "Life is always interesting around Aunt Stormi."

"There may be no more life if we stay." Angela put her face inches from her son's. "Go. Pack. Your. Things."

"We've helped her before." Dakota rarely talked back to his mother, but I could see a full argument brewing.

I glanced at Matt for help. "Do something."

"I agree with your mother." Matt clapped a hand on Dakota's shoulder. "You should go to the cabin."

"The cabin." Cherokee huffed in the way only a teenage girl can. "There is no wifi or cell reception up there. My friends will forget about me."

"I cannot believe that you consider your friends more important than the lives of your family." Tears welled in Angela's eyes. "This is all my fault. Mine and that stupid cream." She raced from the room, returning minutes later with a case of product. "This is going out to the garbage the minute those reporters leave."

"It isn't the product's fault," Mom said. "It's mine. I thought you gave all of that to the police."

"I kept one in my room, just in case." Her look dared us to argue.

The only one not taking blame was me. I should have told Norma I wouldn't help her. It *was* my fault. Once again, I'd jumped in without thinking fully and endangered everyone I love. I would make it right. I'd faced a gun before, I would do it again if it kept my family safe. "It's my fault. I'm sorry."

"This is the craziest family I've ever met." Matt shook his head. "It's a chain of unfortunate events that got you here."

"If I hadn't starting asking questions—"

He held up his hand. "Stop. Just stop. You cannot be

someone you aren't. You have an avid curiosity. Someone murdered Daisy, most likely a competitor, her john … Who knows right now. My concern at this moment is to keep all of you safe."

"I'm not leaving," Dakota said.

"Me either,"Cherokee said.

"I'm the mother and what I say goes." Angela grabbed her daughter's arm. "Go pack."

"No, Mom. Running won't do anything. Tell her Matt. If these people want us that badly, they will find us no matter where we go." She yanked free. "I watch TV. I know this."

"This isn't television," Matt said. "Your mother is right."

"I'll go." I stood. "If I leave, you'll be safe. I'll buy a portable wifi and head to the cabin." Tears clogged my throat as I glanced at the faces of everyone I loved. "I'll go today to buy a four-wheel drive and leave before dark." I marched from the kitchen to my room and closed the door, leaning against the raised panels.

I'd worked so hard to acquire this house. All my life I'd wanted a Victorian beauty to call my own. I moved to the arched window seat and parted the curtains. The reporters had left. I sighed and pulled my suitcase from the closet.

Would this be the last time I stepped into my customized walk-in closet? The last time I would run my fingers along the cool surface of the old-fashioned claw-footed tub?

A knock sounded on my door. "Come in." I pulled open my dresser drawers and grabbed jeans and sweatshirts.

"I'll take you to buy your car." Matt gave me a lopsided grin. "I'm going to ask Greta to stay with you at the cabin." He held up a hand as I started to protest and say that my mother needed her. "It was your mother's idea. A former police woman will be an asset to you. I'll come up there as often as I can get away."

I nodded, letting the tears escape. "Watch out for my

family, Matt."

He wrapped his arms around me. "As if they were my own."

My mind was already trying to find ways to help solve the case so I could come home, if I weren't killed. The sooner we found out who killed Daisy and threatened me, the sooner life could go back to normal.

Matt tilted my face to his. "Ready to buy that car?"

I nodded.

He lowered his head and kissed me, making me forget all my troubles for a few minutes. When he pulled back, I felt more alone than ever before.

"I'll need groceries." We kept the propane tank full but food would only attract critters. Since Dad's death, we barely used the cabin except for the occasional summer vacation from the heat.

Four hours later, I was behind the wheel of a brand new baby blue jeep, Greta in the passenger's seat, Sadie sitting behind me, and the back of the jeep packed to the roof with supplies. In my purse was my pink Glock and a Tazer. I was as ready as I would ever be.

The question was … was I ready enough?

8

After Greta and I unloaded the jeep, I took a cup of coffee onto the cabin's porch, Sadie at my feet, and watched the tree branches move overhead as the wind blew through them. There had been little talking during the unloading. I figured Greta's mind must be as full as mine with what could transpire.

She joined me outside, sitting in the rocker next to the porch swing where I reclined. "Now what?"

"I write on my next book and wait for things to blow over." I sipped my drink. "You shouldn't have come. Your law enforcement days are long over."

She shrugged. "It's good to be in on the action again, even if only as a bodyguard."

I smiled, thinking of the plump late fifties woman as a bodyguard. "I appreciate the company, but you'll be bored."

"I doubt it." She speared me with a glance. "I don't believe for a minute that you intend to sit back and do nothing."

I smiled behind my mug. "I'm working on a plan. Know of any good disguises?"

"I knew it!" She leaned forward. "Now, things are going to get interesting. It almost killed Ann to have to stay behind. I think she knows her daughter very well."

Unfortunately, she does. I prayed Mom wouldn't decide to

take a trip to the cabin. She knew little or nothing about subterfuge. She would lead the bad guys right to me.

"What are you thinking?" Greta scooted her chair closer.

"My original plan was to befriend the gang members. I guess that's out now." I pushed my toes against the wood floor of the porch and set the swing into motion, trying not to pay attention to how cold it was in the mountains. "But, I do want to find out who is responsible for Daisy's death and for the body in my car. In order to do that, I need to ask questions, thus the need for a disguise."

"I have the perfect disguise. We need to head to my place to pick up my van and then to the medical supply store, the thrift store, and then to the costume store." She studied me for a moment. "Wear a hat. That red hair sticks out like a pumpkin in a field of snow."

I dashed inside to grab a beanie, then stuffed my hair under it. Not bad. I looked like a teenager. I sagged my jeans and grabbed my largest sweatshirt. "I'm ready, Grandma."

Greta grinned. "That should work just fine for the trip into town."

The prospect of the trip into town pushed aside how much I would miss my family while away. Even with my current disguise, I had no plans of contacting them or Norma. The less they saw or heard of me, the safer they would be.

After locking Sadie in the cabin, Greta and I got back into the jeep and made the hour drive into town. I parked in front of a strip mall that had seen better days. Cutting the engine, I followed Greta into a medical supply store where she rented a wheelchair. Still unclear as to what her plan was, I followed, without asking a lot of questions, to the thrift store next door.

"Find something to make you look old and frail." Greta headed to a display of wigs.

Did she expect me to wear someone else's hair? Eew!

I flipped through the racks of second hand clothes, settling on a house dress that resembled something my grandmother might have worn. I then grabbed a pack of knee high socks and sensible brown shoes. I'd never worn hand-me-downs before and hoped there would be a chance to wash the clothes before wearing them.

"Stop being a snob," Greta hissed. "I can tell from the prim look on your face how disgusted you are."

"I'm not!"

She gave me the same look Mom used to give me when I argued with her as a child. "We'll throw them in the wash when we pick up my van."

Relieved, I followed her to the cashier, when Greta tossed a short gray wig on top of the things I had chosen. I whipped out my debit card and paid a whopping ten dollars for the whole lot.

We threw the bag into the van and headed across the street to a costume store where Greta purchased a nurse's outfit. Her plan was clicking into place in my head. It might actually work. Who would bother an old lady and her nurse?

"Who are we going to ask questions of?" While I knew we needed to, I had no idea who would be the best to spend time on.

"First, Norma is going to meet us at that restaurant where old people go. Then, we're going to find out who Daisy's friends were, and go from there." Greta opened the passenger door to the jeep. "You'll have to leave this in my garage for a few days."

"Will your van make it up the mountain?"

"Good point. We'll have to drive separately. Where can we leave the van?"

"There's a Wal-Mart on the edge of town. They allow overnight parking."

Greta nodded and instructed me on the way to her house. I

pulled in front of a one-story bungalow with white siding and forest-green shutters. A well-manicured lawn spread from the porch to the street. A cute place that showed pride of ownership. I definitely needed to hire a new gardener.

I followed Greta into a home that smelled of vanilla and lemon. No mess covered the counters, the coffee table was polished to a high sheen, and although the furniture wasn't new, the slipcovers gave a welcoming, homey vibe. I loved it.

"The laundry is off the kitchen. Toss those things in the wash and I'll pour us some tea," Greta said, shrugging off her coat. "We need to make a plan."

By the time I had my thrift store purchases in the wash, Greta had tea poured, cookies on a plate, and a pad of paper and a pencil in front of her. "Now, yes, I used to be a police officer, but I sat behind the desk for fifteen of those twenty years. You probably know as much as I do how to go about questioning people and finding this killer. First, who are our suspects?"

I tossed my beanie on the table and grabbed a chocolate chip cookie from the plate. "Local gang members."

"We need to be more specific. Who was at your sister's facial cream thingamagig?"

I gave her the names of the women present. "Sorry, but I don't have last names."

She tapped the pencil against her teeth. "I might have an idea how we can get that, but it will require a trip to the printing shop. Anyone else?"

"Jamal, Norma's neighbor and his mother Shaunda Brown." I didn't really think Shaunda was a suspect, but I've learned you can't leave anyone off the list.

"That boy has a rap sheet as long as my arm. Assault is at the top of the list, but I can't figure out how he could have gotten his hands on poison ivy this time of year. We need someone interested in botany."

I laughed. "I doubt any of Angela's guests have such a hobby, but how would we find out."

"We get their last names, and I can get their addresses. Don't worry about that. Then, we pay each of them a visit, while they're out working of course."

My eyes widened. "You're willing to break the law?"

"Who said anything about doing anything illegal?" She pasted an innocent look on her face.

"Right." I almost rubbed my hands together. Finally, I had someone with a bit of knowledge in how things in the crime world worked to help me solve a murder.

The washing machine stopped and I went to transfer the clothes to the dryer. I glanced out the back window at a serene view of the mountain. Why would Greta want to risk all this just to help me?

I moved back to my seat. "Why are you helping me?"

"I'm a bored old woman. While I enjoy working in your mother's shop, it doesn't allow much exercising of my gray matter."

"Whatever plan we come up with will make Matt angrier than a hornet locked out of its nest." I drained the last of my tea. I could speak in cute Southern phrases along with Greta.

"He doesn't scare me. I've known him his whole life." Greta placed our glasses in the dishwasher. "He'll spit and sputter, but he'll be grateful for any news we have that takes him a step closer to catching a killer."

Yes, after he lectured me for an hour, then made me feel guilty for worrying him … again.

The dryer buzzed and I hurried to collect our clothes. With my arms full, I rushed back to the kitchen. "Let's drop your van off and head back up the mountain. The more time we spent in town, the higher chance there is someone might see us."

"Smart thinking." Greta followed me outside, locking her door behind us. She yelled out a hello to a neighbor woman across the street. "Nosy old bag," she said with a smile. "Knows everything about everybody."

It wasn't until I backed out of the driveway, tossing a wave in the old woman's direction, that I realized I had forgotten to put my beanie back on. Hopefully, no one would think that I could possibly have been at Greta's house. Few young people in Oak Meadows knew about Greta being a former police officer, and even fewer would think that we would be buddies out on a shopping spree or afternoon visit.

We dropped off the van and Greta climbed into the jeep. She eyed my bare head and shook hers. "We've got to be better about disguising you."

"I could dye it." Please say it wasn't necessary. I loved my red hair.

"No, a wig or hat should do just fine." She buckled her seat belt.

I drove back to the cabin as a light rain began to fall. A fire in the fireplace sounded like a good idea.

I stopped in front of the cabin and stared through the window at Matt, who frowned from the driver's seat of his car. Why hadn't he called me? He climbed out and met us on the porch.

"The point of the cabin," he said. "Is for the two of you to stay here where it's safe."

"Don't fret." Greta patted him on the shoulder. "We headed to my place to pick up a few things."

He chewed the inside of his lip. "Next time, call me and I'll get you anything you need. I'm counting on you to keep an eye on Stormi."

"I'm right here," I sang out as I unlocked the door. "You can talk to me."

"I am keeping a very close eye on our girl. Don't worry."

Greta smiled, tossed me a wink, and bustled into the cabin ahead of me and Matt. "Since you're here, you might as well stay for supper."

Matt slung his arm around my shoulder. "Sounds good." He put his mouth next to ear, his breath tickling the short hairs at the nape of my neck. "Your cats miss you. So do I."

I giggled. "I haven't even been gone a full day."

"Almost. The sun is sitting low on the horizon." He straightened and glanced around the cabin. "I bet it gets really dark out here."

"Very much."

"We need to install motion detection lights and better locks on the doors. Maybe a security system." He paced the living room, even going as far as to peer up the chimney. Who did he expect? Santa Claus? "Yes, I think that's a good idea."

Great. Every deer that strolled across the lawn would light the place up like Fort Knox. Plus, Matt knew how bad I was at setting my house alarm. He'd know the first time Greta and I headed into town.

Our plan was in danger of failing before it got started.

9

Matt made a few phone calls and had a crew of technicians to the cabin within the hour. He seemed as pleased as if he had given me a great gift. I suppose he had. After all, he only wanted to protect me. Still, his chivalrous actions would make it difficult for Greta and I to do some snooping.

Greta watched the proceedings with a secretive smile on her face as she set bowls of canned stew on the table. "Come and eat."

Once we sat at a small wooden table, I felt comfortable enough to ask Matt some questions. I was glad to see him and didn't want him to think gleaning him for information was the only reason for my pleasure. "Any identification on the body in my car?"

"I can't give you his name, yet, but it is a gang member. The young man was shot in the head and then deposited in your car." He gave me a shrewd look. "It's a warning."

"Why not just send me a note?" I set my spoon beside my bowl. Someone didn't have to die for me to get the message. Appetite gone, I reached for my can of diet soda. "Anything else cleared up?"

He shook his head. "We need to infiltrate the gang in order to move this case along, and I don't see that happening."

I tried not to look at Greta. Matt was a perceptive man and

57

would know from a glance that we had something planned.

From the sound of her spoon clinking against her bowl, she was focused on her simple meal. I set my supper on the floor for Sadie. The chances of the gang finding out about the family cabin were slim. After all, I had no gang dealings. They didn't know me or my family. The closest I came to knowing them was giving them a pizza. Surely, that wouldn't put me in their cross-hairs. So why were they focused on me?

"Any idea how the poison ivy got into Angela's face cream?" I picked up the empty bowl. Sadie had inhaled the stew.

"No. Someone must be growing the stuff, but why? It isn't ornamental or useful in any way." Matt pushed his own empty bowl to the side. "We're looking for a horticulturist."

I doubted any of the prostitutes had time for such pursuits, but wouldn't discount the idea completely. We had the pieces of the puzzle, they just weren't fitting together. The past year had shown I was good at puzzles. We'd figure it out; hopefully, sooner rather than later.

"Thanks for the dinner." Matt stood. "Here is the code for the alarm." He handed me a slip of paper and a remote. "The remote operates the television, which gives you video surveillance of each side of your house. Tomorrow, I'll bring pizza." He tilted my face to his and kissed me. "Try to get some sleep. You look done in." He smiled and left.

"How are we going to figure out who is growing poison ivy?" I cleared the table, stacking the dishes in the sink.

"We're going to ask questions." Greta filled the sink with hot water and added soap. "You're going to be a nosy old woman worried about the spiritual needs of today's youth. You're going to talk about hobbies and God, which will either alienate or endear those boys to you."

"They'll recognize me."

"Not with the makeup you'll be wearing. You'll look every year of your seventy-two years." Greta chuckled. "Before joining law enforcement, I dabbled in theatre. This will work."

I hoped so. We needed a huge break. While I loved the cabin, it was for vacation, not a place to hide. "You do realize that anyone can approach the cabin from four different directions, three of which are covered with trees?" The surveillance cameras will pick up any movement, but by then, anyone intending to do me harm will already be on the property.

"I don't think anyone can find out where you are unless they are told. Your family won't talk, will they?"

"Not unless their lives are threatened." If someone said they would hurt one of her children, then Angela would spill her guts. Not that I blamed her. I'd do the same if I had children.

"Don't let things get you down." Greta handed me a bowl to dry. "We'll catch Daisy's killer and protect you at the same time. It isn't a surprise to God that we're out here."

I nodded, hoping it wasn't my time to be called "home". "I think I'm going to get a bit of writing done and check my emails." I left her to do the dishes and headed to one of the two bedrooms.

I'd set my laptop on the dresser and waited for a very slow internet to dial up. While my phone had a WiFi I could hook the laptop to, it wasn't as fast as I was used to. I glanced at the shuttered window, hating that it wasn't safe enough to watch the sunset over the trees. I didn't see the reason for the windows to be boarded. Matt hadn't said we had to stay inside, just out of the city. I opened the window and pushed the shutters wide. If I wanted privacy, I'd use the curtains.

Sadie whined at the door. I grabbed her leash off the dresser and grabbed my coat. The poor dog couldn't be expected to stay cooped up inside all the time.

"Take your gun," Greta called as I headed for the door.

I sighed and pulled my Glock from my purse, then slipped it into the waistband of my jeans. One year ago, I was nothing more than a romance novelist who wanted to be left alone with my cats. Since then, I'd stumbled over a dead body, literally, became owner of said body's giant scaredy-cat dog, then had a crazy woman stalk me because I wasn't writing my books fast enough. Now, this. I couldn't help but wonder if changing to the mystery genre had been a bad move. Maybe I should have chosen erotica, eew, but they didn't seem to have insane fans disturbing their peaceful lives. Maybe she needed to ask Sarah Thompson if she had any kooks bothering her.

Brr, it was cold. I let Sadie loose, commanded her to stay, and pulled my coat tighter around me. Looping her leash around my wrist again, I strolled the perimeter of the property. The crisp air cleared my head and woke my appetite.

A breeze blew the branches of the leafless trees, the sound like whispers from a graveyard. The lowering sun cast shadows that sent my heart into overdrive. "Hurry up, Sadie. I'm getting creeped out."

How dare this unknown person make me afraid of one of my most favorite places? Every summer of my childhood had been spent swimming in the lake on the other side of the trees. I refused to let someone destroy my pleasant memories. I headed back to the cabin and sat on the steps while Sadie did her business.

The sun finally disappeared over the horizon, casting the area into darkness until Sadie moved, then the yard lit up like a football stadium. I sighed and headed inside, calling for Sadie to follow.

Greta sat on the sofa, the television on. "This is pretty

cool. I watched you walk around the entire yard."

It wouldn't have done much good if someone would have been waiting for me. There was no way Greta would have gotten to me in time. I refilled Sadie's water dish and joined Greta on the sofa. "Is there anything else on television."

She laughed. "Without cable, no. I'll have to read."

"You make it sound like a death sentence."

"Not one of my favorite past times." She set down the remote, leaving the TV on. "I did bring some knitting. Maybe I'll work on my scarf."

Figuring my computer had to be booted up by then, I went back to my room. Over one hundred emails waited for a response. I scanned through and deleted the ones I didn't want to read and opened one from my agent.

"Just a reminder about your book signing this Saturday. Good luck."

How could I have forgotten. I sent an email to her and one to the bookstore saying I had had a family emergency and would need to reschedule. I would explain more to my agent when I was no longer in hiding.

Another email, this one from Sarah Thompson, erotica writer with a twisted mind, asked where I was. She needed to talk to me about a plot that wouldn't fall into place. While I didn't mind helping other writers, her stuff grossed me out. I replied that I was out of town on vacation and would connect with her in a week.

Now that the emails I needed to take care of were out of the way, I pulled up my latest manuscript. The blank page taunted me. I'd never been able to concentrate under stress. Instead, my mind drifted to which of our suspects would be the most likely to have access to poison ivy in January. Not one of them seemed a good candidate.

"Stormi, come here," Greta called from the living room.

I joined her and witnessed a fox scurrying along the tree

line, highlighted by the motion lights. "I guess we'll see a lot of wildlife."

"I think so." She sighed. "The time out here is going to drag. I've done stakeouts before that had more action."

"Let's plan what questions we're going to ask tomorrow." I sat on the other end of the sofa.

"Good idea. Remember, the focus is on pretending to witness to people while snooping into their private lives. We have to find out who had a grudge against Daisy and who is into plants."

"I'm not a very good actress." I plucked at the canary yellow skein of yarn between Greta and I.

"No pressure, but you'll have to be. Your life could depend on it."

"Matt would say that saving my life means staying put here."

"But, you can't do that."

I shook my head. "Nope. I've never been very good at letting others solve my problems." As evidenced in the past.

Why couldn't I sit back like a good girl and let the police handle the danger? Because the not knowing what was going on would drive me crazy. I was a poor, pathetic, sick-in-the-head writer of romantic mysteries and romance novels. I wanted to add an element of truth to my stories.

I sighed. I hadn't even had time lately to research love scenes with Matt.

"You look like someone ran over your dog." Greta picked up her knitting.

"Just thinking of Matt's kisses."

"That ought to make you smile, not sigh like the weight of the world is on your shoulders."

"We haven't had a lot of time to work on our relationship."

She grinned. "When he comes tomorrow, I'll make myself

scarce in my room and you two can set the sofa on fire."

I giggled. "We keep our relationship very proper."

"Too bad. That man is some good eye-candy. If I were twenty years younger, I'd give you some competition. Now, there are some twinkies in the pantry. Why don't you grab us each one?"

"So cliché!" I smiled, wishing we had doughnuts.

I found the box stuffed behind some dry cereal and pulled out two of the lard filled cakes. Sadie's attention transferred from what I was getting to the back door. The hair on the back of her neck bristled. I closed the pantry door as quietly as possible and parted the curtains over the window.

A face in a ski mask stared back at me. I screamed.

10

I yanked the door open and pulled my nephew inside. The alarm screamed. I punch in the numbers to disarm it."Dakota Nelson, what in the world are you doing here?"

Greta dashed into the kitchen, her gun drawn. "Boy, I could have killed you."

"How did you know it was me?" Dakota pulled off his ski mask.

"Because I bought that mask for you for Christmas." I bopped him in the back of the head. "Now, answer my question."

"It's boring at home. I thought you could use my help. Twinkies!" He grabbed the ones in my hand and sat at the kitchen table.

"No way." Greta set her gun on the counter and snatched them back. "Not until we're done talking to you. How did you get here?"

"I had a friend drop me off. Don't worry. I swore him to secrecy." He glanced at the television. "Cool. Cameras. See? You need me. I can help watch. We can take shifts."

"Oh, Dakota." I shook my head, taking a seat across the table from him. "Coming here has put us in danger."

"No, my friend won't say anything. I only told him we were spending the weekend at the cabin. He doesn't know what's going on so can't say anything to hurt us." He tapped his temple with his forefinger. "I thought about it first."

"Not very well." My sister was going to have a fit when she found out. "We need to take you home."

"I'll just come back. Let me help, please." He gave me the look kids who want something are so famous for giving.

"It's past your bedtime," I said, for lack of anything else.

"Puh-leese. Can I have the Twinkies now?"

Greta tossed them to him. "It's against my better judgement for him to stay, but it's too late to drive him home now."

"I'll call Angela." I huffed and went to my room to fetch my cell phone.

I dialed her number. "Dakota is here," I said the minute she answered.

"What do you mean he's there?" Her shrill voice threatened to pierce my eardrum. "He's spending the night with his friend, Carl."

"No, he had his friend drop him off here. He said he was bored."

"You had better not let my boy get shot." Click.

That went better than I'd thought. What were we going to do with Dakota when we went snooping in the morning?

"Your mother hung up on me," I said, joining the other two in the living room. I collapsed in the easy hair and glanced at the television which the other two were totally engrossed in. "This is getting ridiculous." I got to my feet and opened the front door. "Cherokee! Get in here." Once she was inside, I set the alarm.

"This is a regular family reunion," Greta said. "Doesn't anyone respect boundaries?"

"Not in my family."

"Grandma's coming," Cherokee said, plopping on the sofa between Greta and her brother. She jumped back up like she'd been bit and pulled a knitting needle from the cushions.

"You could kill someone with these things. Grandma's car is having trouble getting up the road."

Matt was going to have a coronary. I dialed his number on my phone.

"Miss me already?"

"Yes." I bit my bottom lip. "There's no easy way to tell you this, but my entire family has arrived at the cabin. Except for Angela, that is."

"Explain." His voice hardened.

"I didn't invite them. They just showed up. Dakota said he was bored. I haven't asked Mom and Cherokee why they're here yet." I closed my eyes and leaned my head against the back of the chair. A massive headache was knocking, asking to come in.

The alarm shrilled again on Mom's entrance. "I've got to go. See you tomorrow." I hung up before Matt could protest and hurried to punch in the code.

"The alarm thing again?" Mom frowned. "Must we be annoyed here and at home?"

"It's for your safety." Greta stood and helped Mom with her armload of groceries. It looked as if she'd bought enough for a year's stay.

"What are all of you doing here?" I planted my fists on my hips. "What about the shop, Mom?"

"I took a vacation. I'm worn out, too. It was a lot of work getting the orders done without Greta so I could take a few days off." She plopped a cardboard box on the table. "Can you get the suitcases, Dakota?"

He sighed. "Is my mom coming, too? Because I can do a lot more if she isn't here."

"I have no idea, sweetie." Mom kissed his cheek, which he promptly wiped off, then gave him a shove to the door.

"Fifteen-year-old boys don't like kisses on their cheeks from their grandmother," I said heading outside to help my nephew.

"My grandson will never outgrow my kisses!"

Dakota leaned against the van. "Mom will be here. You know that, right? And she's the most paranoid person I know."

"That's how mothers are where their children are concerned." Not that I had personal experience. I leaned next to him. "While I love all of you very much, I wish you wouldn't have come."

"You can't fight this on your own. Just like the other times, family sticks together." He cocked his head and peered up at me. "How do you keep getting mixed up in these things?"

"Luck, I guess." I pushed away from the van. "Let's get unloaded."

Three suitcases later, my head still pounded. The bright security lights in my eyes as I headed for the cabin didn't help either. I set the suitcases inside the door, reset the alarm, and wondered where everyone was going to sleep.

The question was answered the moment I walked in the door. Mom was sharing my room, Cherokee had claimed Greta's room to share with her mother upon her inevitable arrival, Greta had the pull out sofa, and Dakota was already spreading a sleeping bag on the floor.

"What's the plan?" Mom asked over her shoulder as she put away groceries. "I know you have one."

Greta filled Mom in while I searched for a bottle of ibuprofen. I found one in the bathroom that had expired six months ago. With a shrug, I took three.

"What do you want me to do?" Mom looked like a child on their birthday.

"Nothing," I said, joining them again. "You were supposed to stay home. Since you didn't, you, and the others, will be staying here."

"No." Mom pouted. "I want to do something. If you don't allow me to, I'll follow you. I can be incognito if I have to."

"You're about as incognito as the proverbial pink elephant." I plopped into a chair. She was right. She would only follow. "Fine. But you're the driver of the van. You'll dress like a man and wear one of Dakota's beanies. You. Will. Stay. In. The. Van." This was a bad idea.

"You, daughter of mine, are no fun."

"Mom's here." Cherokee stared out the window. "She looks mad."

The ibuprofen was doing nothing for my headache. I disarmed the alarm before it went off and opened the door for Angela.

"You're a menace," she said, pushing past me. "I ought to pack up my kids and move out of your house where you can't be a bad influence on them."

"Go ahead." There were times when I would like nothing more. This was one of those times.

"Oh, you'd like that, wouldn't you?" Her face darkened.

"Yes." I tilted my head to the side and smiled. "You're sharing a room with your daughter." I could not believe her attitude. I was renovating the attic into a private space for her and this was the thanks I got.

My cell phone rang. "Yeah?"

"Is this a bad time?" Matt's soft laughter eased a bit of my stress.

"My entire family is here." I stepped into the far corner of the kitchen to find some privacy. "I almost want the gang to find me."

"That bad, huh?"

"Worse." I plopped into a chair. "At least at home I could hide in my office. Won't it look suspicious that we've all left?"

"Yes, it will. I will try and convince the rest of your

family to return home when I visit tomorrow. Why aren't you in bed?"

"Seriously? I have to share a room, and a bed, with my mother."

"Poor thing." He laughed again. "I called because I was on my way home when Angela sped past me. I figured she was headed your way and was hoping to warn you."

"Thanks, but you're too late." I stood again and leaned back against the refrigerator. "Is there somewhere secret me and Greta could go?"

"I'll see what I can do. Talk to you tomorrow." Click.

"Come on, Sadie." I opened the back door and stepped outside, wishing immediately that I had grabbed my jacket. I wrapped my arms around my middle and waited.

Behind me, I heard the unmistakable sound of the lock engaging on the door. "Hey!" I banged on the window. "I'm out here!"

"Sorry." Mom grinned as she opened the door. "I should have looked."

I hugged and trudged past her. "I'm going to bed."

"I'll come tuck you in a bit."

I rolled my eyes. I guessed sharing a bed invited certain childhood rituals. How on God's green earth were Greta and I going to get away in the morning without a traveling circus?

Since it took forever for my laptop to come alive on the mountain, I left it connected and closed the cover before dropping my clothes on the floor, donning flannel pajamas, and climbing into bed.

Footsteps going past my door alerted me to the fact the others were also turning in for the night. I glanced at the time on my phone. Eleven fifty p.m. I was going to be a bear in the morning, and actually felt sorry for any gang members who might say the wrong thing to me.

"Are you mad?" Mom shuffled into the room by the light of a flashlight.

"Yep." I rolled over and faced the wall.

"Don't you think the family should stick together?"

"Not in this particular instance." Why did she not understand? "Your coming here has put everyone in danger. I'm looking for somewhere else to go, and I won't be telling you."

"You're acting like a child." The bed sagged as she sat on the edge.

"How so?" I sat up. "How is being worried about the people I love acting like a child?"

"We should be able to make our own decisions." She turned off the flashlight and lay down. "We're well aware of the danger and don't want you to face it alone."

"I can't focus on what I need to do if you're with me."

"You aren't supposed to be *doing* anything."

"Are you going to tell Matt?" I lay on my pillow and pulled the blankets to my chin.

"Not if you let me go and keep an eye on you."

"How will that work if we're both dead?" A fist grabbed a hold of my heart and squeezed.

"We won't be. We have a great Protector."

"Yeah, it's a good thing the Bible says He looks over the foolish."

"Goodnight, sweetie."

"Goodnight, Mom."

Soon, gentle snores filled the room. I lay on my back and stared through the darkness toward the ceiling. Having any of them come along in the morning was stupid and irresponsible. I needed to figure out something they could do and still feel as if they were helping me. Something that kept them out of harm's way.

I could send the kids to the library to see what they could

dig up on the local gangs. They only had a week left before the winter break ended and they started back to school. Angela had either taken a leave of absence from work and would go to the library to watch her kids, or she planned on making the long drive each day to her job as receptionist at the police station. Which, could actually be of some benefit. She could keep me posted on any rumors floating around.

That left Mom. I didn't need to ask where she would be.

11

Mom squeezed her ample chest into one of Dakota's sweatshirts, hid her curls under a tattered beanie, and headed out the door to the van. Greta and I exchanged an amused glance. I set the alarm and headed for the back seat. Angela had agreed to dropping the kids off at the library before heading to work. We would all discuss at supper any information we found.

"Where are we going?" Mom started the van, despite how it struggled to traverse mountain roads, and glanced in the rearview mirror.

"Head to Melrose and park in front of the old video store." I clicked my seatbelt into place. "If we want to be realistic, we'll need to talk to people who aren't our suspects."

"That makeup job Greta did really makes you unrecognizable. You look just like your grandmother."

"It itches like the dickens." Blessed with smooth, porcelain skin, Greta had applied what felt like inches of pancake makeup in order to age me by about forty years. Greta wore a starched white nurse's uniform. I doubt Matt could recognize us unless he got close. I rested my head against the seat back and took a nap until we arrived in town.

"Wake up, old lady." Mom pounded the back of Greta's seat. "We're here."

Greta was already opening the back of the van and

removing the wheelchair. I blinked against the grit in my eyes from lack of sleep, and reached for the door.

"Nope." Greta rolled the wheelchair toward me. "You're infirm. I have to help you. Acting, Stormi!"

"I forgot for a second." I held out my arm and let her guide me into the wheelchair. She plopped a stack of church fliers on my lap.

"I got these from my church. Thought it would be easier than making them ourselves, not that we remembered in the hoopla last night."

"Good idea." I yawned and glanced in the van's side mirror. Everything still looked like it was in place after my short nap. I took a deep breath to steady my nerves. It was now or never. "Onward, Lucy."

"Lucy?"

"That's your name or the day. Mine is Edna. Mom, do not get out of the van for any reason. If Greta and I run into trouble, call Matt. Do. Not. Get. Out. Of. The. Van."

"I heard you the first time." She moved her seat back so she was hidden by the side panel and rolled up all the windows.

Fine. Better mad and alive than happy and dead. I put a hand on the Bible tracts so they wouldn't blow away and hunched over under the knitted shawl across my shoulders.

An hour later, my back hurt and we'd offended more people than we spoke with. A few young boys took the papers and turned them into paper airplanes. It was time to hit Norma's friends and Jamal's group of friends. My stomach sank to my knees. If I said the wrong thing, or one of them recognized me, the gig was up and the danger to me and my family had doubled.

"There's Ginger." Greta pushed me toward the skinny redhead who leaned against a lamp post.

"May we talk with you, dear?" I did my best to sound old.

"Are you one of those do-gooders?" Ginger straightened and eyed the tract as if it would bite her. "I'm not interested."

"How about a little conversation?"

She cocked her head. "My time is worth money."

Darn. I hadn't thought of that. I dug in the large purple bag Greta insisted I hang from the handles of the wheelchair and pulled out five dollars. "A dollar a minute?"

"It's your money."

"What do you do in your spare time?"

Her eyes narrowed. "Why?"

"Well," I shrugged. "If you have a lot of it, you need a hobby. Something that fulfills you."

"I'm taking classes in flower arrangements. I want to be a florist." She squared her shoulders as if daring me to say something derogatory.

Instead, I had to fight to keep my composure. "That's wonderful."

She smiled. "Yeah, me a couple of the other girls are all dabbling in flowers. That one over there?" She pointed at Ivy. "She actually has a greenhouse behind where her mother lives. That other girl," she pointed at Lacey. "She experiments with making hybrids. The only one of us that isn't interested in flowers or plants is Sissy. She writes nasty books.

"So, see? We all have outside interests. You don't need to concern yourself."

"Would your friends talk to us?" Excitement made my hands tremble. I clutched the arms of the wheelchair to steady them. The papers in my lap fluttered, then danced off my lap and down the street.

Ginger tottered on her stilettos and captured five of them. "Sorry about that. Maybe some poor soul will find one and read it." She handed me the papers. "You need to move on now. I have to work. Mornings are slow as it is."

"God bless you, my child." It seemed the appropriate thing to say, and I meant it.

Greta and I moved down the sidewalk to Ivy and Sissy. Down the street, I spotted Jamal and his group rough housing. Spiders skittered up and down my spine at the thought of questioning them.

I repeated my spiel to the women.

"Yeah, I like plants, so what?" Ivy crossed her arms.

"She's always fiddling in her greenhouse," Sissy said. "It's a waste of time."

"Says you." Ivy bumped her with her hip.

"Have you created anything of interest?"

She peered into my face. "Why do you want to know? Do I know you?"

I shook my head, trying to look haggard. "I've always loved flowers."

She didn't look as if she believed me, but hitched one shoulder. "I've created a new species of roses, I think. This is a tough business I'm in. Playing with flowers relaxes me." She glanced at Jamal, who leaned, one foot planted on the brick wall behind him. "You two need to move on before we get into trouble."

"Maybe we'll speak to those young men before we leave," I said.

"I wouldn't, but it's your neck." Ivy and Sissy walked away, motioning for Lacey to follow them.

"So far so good," I told Greta. "Are you sure you want to talk to the boys?"

"We're already here. You'd make a good undercover detective, Stormi. Your performance has been flawless."

I wanted to throw up. "Thanks."

We moved slowly down the sidewalk toward Jamal. My heart rate accelerated to the point to where I felt as if I were in cardiac arrest. My mouth dried like the land in a drought.

Jamal pushed off the wall and approached us. "What are you two old ladies doing messing with those girls? You want their pimps down on you?"

"No, we're offering them salvation." I lifted a trembling hand and offered him a tract. "And, we were discussing flowers."

"For real?" He disregarded the offered paper. "You got guts coming here, that's for sure. Most of you church people are too afraid. Are you scared?" He put his face close to mine.

Where was the young man willing to share a bit of conversation with me? The one who thanked me for a pizza?

"I'm an old woman. What do I have to be afraid of?" Him. Everything.

"Death." He straightened, his gaze focused on my face.

Could he see through my disguise? It was time to leave. "Lucy, I'm ready for my nap."

"Good idea, old woman." Jamal put a hand on the wheelchair, stopping us. "Those girls don't need hope and encouragement. They leave their pimps, they'll get hurt. You mind your own business."

"Others have left the profession."

"And bear the scars."

I needed to talk to Norma. What scars did she carry?

He leaned over, his mouth next to my ear. He sniffed, then gave me a straight-lipped smile. "Where's my pizza, Miss Nelson? You shouldn't come without bearing gifts."

I turned my head, my eyes clashing with his. I waited to see whether he would keep our secret.

"Stop asking questions. I can't keep protecting you." He straightened, gave us the finger, which sent his friends howling with laughter, and joined them.

"Let's get back to the van, Greta. Quickly."

She practically ran on the way back, ignoring ribald

comments tossed our way. At the van, I didn't wait for her assistance. I yanked open the door and leaped inside. She folded up the wheelchair, tossed it inside, and dashed back to her seat.

"How in the world did he recognize you?" She asked, staring out the window.

"Who? Who recognized you?" Mom started the engine.

"Jamal. He warned me again to stay out of things." I could hardly buckle my seatbelt, my hands shook so hard.

Mom squealed tires getting us off Melrose Street. "What did you do wrong?"

"She didn't do anything wrong. He smelled her," Greta said.

"That's disgusting."

"I use a particular brand of body wash." I never thought someone could recognize me by the scent. Surely, other people washed with it. "He said he can't keep protecting me. What did he mean by that?"

"Someone else is after you and he keeps stopping them?" Mom whipped the wheel right, taking us to the freeway.

"You can slow down now," Greta said. "No one is following us."

"I'm not slowing down until we get to the cabin." She pressed the accelerator, shooting us down the off ramp.

"Nothing will matter if we die in a car wreck." Greta clutched the handle over her head.

"Uh-oh." Mom glanced in the rearview mirror.

"What?" I glanced behind us.

"We are being followed."

"Speed up!" I yanked off my wig and grabbed some hand wipes from under the seat. If I was going to die, I wanted to die as Stormi.

"I'll try to outrun them." The van shook as Mom increased the speed.

"This old girl isn't meant to go this fast," Greta said.

"You or the van?" Mom glanced again at the mirror.

"Both!"

"Wait. Pull over." I recognized the car. "It's Matt."

"Do you really want me to stop?" Mom's eyes widened. "You know what he's going to say."

"He knows where we're headed." We might as well get the lecture over with.

"Okay." Gravel crunched under the tires as Mom pulled onto the shoulder.

Matt stopped behind us, thrust open his door, and marched to the driver side window. He motioned for Mom to roll the window down. "Do I even want to know?"

"Nope." Mom smiled. "We'll just be on our way, then."

He glanced in the back seat. "What's on your face?"

"Uh, makeup?" I rubbed at my cheek, studying my face in the mirror between Mom and Greta.

Matt sighed. "What have you three been up to? Greta, I thought you knew better than to let Stormi off the mountain."

"We had questions that needed answers." She gave him a hard look. "Stormi is a born investigator. We found out a lot of information today."

"You could have been spotted."

"They were." Mom nodded. "Jamal warned Stormi to stop asking questions."

Matt straightened and ran his hands through his hair, muttering words I couldn't catch. He turned back to the van. "Get out, Stormi."

I shook my head. Was I stupid?

"Get out of the van."

I felt like a child about to be spanked. "Not until you calm down."

"I am calm!"

"No, you're not."

He took a deep breath. "Please, get out of the van."

I slid over and opened the door. Matt hurried to the other side and pulled me into his arms. His heart beat fast under my cheek. He held me at arm's length. "I knew you would try something. I've been following you all morning. What are you thinking?"

"That I want to catch Daisy's killer?"

"Stormi Nelson." He unhooked handcuffs from his belt. "I'm placing you under arrest for impeding an investigation." He clicked the cold steel around my wrists.

12

Matt led me to the passenger front seat. I lifted my chin. "Since you've arrested me like a common criminal, I'll sit in the back, thank you."

"Suit yourself." He opened the back door and, placing a hand on my head, guided me inside.

"Are you crazy?" Mom stood in front of him, hands on her hips. "Uncuff her this instant."

"Not until she comes to her senses." He brushed past her and Greta, and slid behind the wheel of his car. He slammed the door and roared onto the highway.

I blinked back tears and stared out the window. From the corner of my eye, I caught Matt glancing in the rearview mirror. Well, he could look all he wanted. I was not going to speak to him.

"This is for your own good," he said.

"Yes, Dad." I was being childish and knew it. I also didn't care. I was a grown woman who intended to protect herself and her family at all costs. How dare my *boyfriend* step in to interfere? I chose to ignore the fact he was a cop, which gave him the right, but I was too mad to care.

At the police station, he marched me to a cell. The other officers watched with amused looks as Matt locked the door.

"Hey!" I banged my cuffs on the door. "Aren't you going to book me? You can't keep me here if you don't." I flopped onto a concrete bench that circled the cell. Odors of vomit and body sweat assailed me. I tried breathing through my mouth, which sounded like I had a snorkeling tube shoved between my lips.

Three women, one twice my size, and two who were obviously in the same profession as Ivy and her friends, stared at me as if I were a bug on the wall. How many prostitutes did this town have? I couldn't recall any while I was growing up. Oak Meadows needed to get rid of the gang element.

"What did you do?" The big woman peered into my face. "You look as sweet as ice cream."

"I supposedly interfered in a police investigation." I saw no need to lie.

She shook her head. "I'm Billie. You're right, though, they do need to book you in order to keep you here."

"He wants to teach me a lesson." I stared at a spot on the floor that looked suspiciously like blood.

"Will it work?"

"No."

She laughed, the sound loud and booming. "You go, girl. I know who you are. You're that writer that solves crimes. Am I right?"

I nodded, peeking up at her. Was I in danger by answering her question truthfully?

"What are you trying to find out?" She motioned the other women closer. "Ain't nobody gonna know if we tell you anything. Not in here anyway. Just make sure you put me in one of your books."

Did everyone want to be in a book? "Okay. What do you do for a living, Billie?"

"I'm a truck driver arrested for transporting questionable goods." She laughed again. "There's a lot more money in contraband than there is in food."

"I don't usually break the law, other than sticking my nose where the police don't think it belongs."

"Of course you don't, sweetie. Ask me anything." Billie crossed her arms, her muscles as big as any mans. She didn't look like someone you wanted against you.

"Why do you want to help me?"

She shrugged. "What else am I going to do? I can't post bail. I'm here until the judge sentences me and they move me to a more permanent home."

Good point. I explained about Daisy's death and how I was looking to find someone with experience in horticulture. I didn't want to give names, in case I influenced their answers. I also left out where I was living and the morning's epic failure. Once I finished, I leaned back against the wall and watched the wheels turn in the women's heads.

"I don't have much use for women of that profession," Billie said, raising a hand against the other women's protests. "But, to each their own, no offense. Ladies, do you have any clues for our mystery writer? Let's solve this case right here, right now."

One of the prostitutes, a girl who looked no older than Cherokee, whispered. "I don't want to tell you my name. That can get me killed, but that Ivy girl who works Melrose Street is bad news. Don't mess with her. She'll also take up for any of her friends. She has a greenhouse with all kinds of stuff in it."

This wasn't new. "Anything else?"

"She's the head gang leaders woman. If you want to know what's going on, and you're willing to risk the danger, then you need to befriend her."

The other girls nodded. "No one knows the leader's real name," the same girl said, "but he goes by Stinger."

"What does he look like?" I asked.

"No one has ever seen him, at least not that they know

of." She retreated to the corner of the cell as footsteps pounded down the hall.

Matt, his face as red as my newest pair of ballet flats, which were the shade of cherries, dragged Maryann, his sister and my best friend to the cell. "Spend some time in here to cool off."

She yanked free. "Gladly." She sailed through the door after he opened it. "Hello, Stormi."

Matt cast me a pained glance. I looked away. "What are you doing here, Maryann?"

"I assaulted a police officer," she giggled. "Once I heard you were in the slammer, I demanded Matt release you. When he refused, I slapped him." She plopped on the bench beside me. "I feel bad, kind of. He's only doing what he thinks will protect you, but for crying out loud, isn't here another way?"

"It isn't so bad," I said. "Billie and the others are answering some questions for me."

"Great. I found out some things, too." She proceeded to tell me that the police department had hired some men to go undercover and try to get the gang out of our city. "I don't know who they are, and I don't want to. That would be dangerous for them."

"How did you find this out?"

"I'm the best eavesdropper in the world, remember?" She smiled at the other women before turning back to me. "Your mom and Greta are in the front causing a ruckus as we speak. We'll be out of here by nightfall, or Matt isn't my brother."

My suspect list was growing, and I was no closer to finding out who killed Daisy than I was the day she was murdered. "Does anyone here know of why Daisy might have been killed?"

"I might." One of the other women, this one way too old to be walking the streets, said, "Rumor on the streets is that she saw something she shouldn't have and made too much noise."

"What did she see?"

She shrugged. "Girl, if I knew that, I'd be dead, too, but rumor has it, she saw some underhanded dealings in the gang."

"That happens all the time," Billie said. "So what was different this time?"

"I don't know. It has something to do with Stinger."

I met Maryann's gaze. It turned out, getting thrown behind bars might have been the most productive thing to have happened to me since Daisy's death. "I don't know you women, but I hope that anything said in this cell doesn't leave here."

"Definitely," Billie said. "We'll all be in danger if it does." She narrowed her eyes. "If I find out someone talks, they'll have to deal with me, and if I'm locked up, well, I have a lot of friends."

"No need for threats." I put my hand on Billie's arm. "I'm going to find Daisy's killer, hopefully before I'm dead. I won't say a word about where I get my information. Other than, Billie, who asked to be in my book, the other three of you don't exist. Billie, I'll change your name and profession, but you'll know who you are. Thank you."

"One more thing." The youngest girl spoke up. "I've never seen Ivy turn a trick. She seems more of a watchdog to me and that Sissy rarely leaves her side."

Another good fact to know. I looked up as Matt approached the cell. "Stormi, Maryann, you're free to go. Ann and Greta won't leave me alone until you're out." He unlocked the door.

"Looks like your little plan didn't work." I shoved past him.

"I'll talk to you later," he said, his voice stern.

"We'll see. I have a headache and plan to go to bed early." Right after I write down everything I learned that day.

I rushed to where my Mom and Greta waited. "Thanks." I bent close to Mom's ear. "Wait until you hear what I found out."

"Go home, Maryann," Matt said behind me. "You, too, Stormi. We'll talk later."

I shrugged. I'm sure we would talk, or rather he would lecture and I would halfway listen. I knew it pained him that trouble followed me, but I didn't ask Daisy be killed, or to be threatened. I had every intention of staying out of her murder until that threat happened. Now that it had, I'd been exiled to the mountain. I was determined to solve this case and get back into my daily routine of writing.

At the van, I turned around. Matt watched from the front steps of the police department. The hurt expression on his face was almost my undoing. I tossed him a wave and a sad smile. He was right. I shouldn't be involved. But yet again, the trouble came to me. I didn't go looking for it, but I wasn't one to sit back and wait while an already overworked police department tried to solve the case.

I climbed into the back seat, willing to let Mom drive and stared out the window. Things were growing more and more complicated. While I was happy not to actually be arrested, I could have asked a few more questions of my new acquaintances. Oh, well. They'd given me a few clues to follow up on.

Who was Stinger? How was Jamal involved in all this, and why did he continue to warn me? Why should he care? Did his mother know he was involved in the gang? How could she not?

I decided a visit to Shaunda might be on the agenda. I would really like to find a way to get her son free from the gang's clutches. What would that entail? Would it be dangerous to the boy? There was so much I didn't know. When this was all over, I'd ask Matt how to free Jamal.

I was so lost in my thoughts, the hour drive to the cabin seemed more like ten minutes. When we arrived, I headed straight to the shower. I could still feel the oil from the pancake makeup on my face, not to mention the rank odors of the jail cell.

After turning the water to hot, I shed my out-of-date clothes and waited for the shower to heat. My heart lay heavy in my chest, fearing I couldn't repair the damage done to mine and Matt's relationship. I needed to apologize and plead my case.

Hopefully, he could see my side of things.

13

I got my chance that night after supper. The family had just cleaned the dishes, and sat back at the table, when Matt arrived. Knowing the alarm code, he let himself in and disarmed it.

"Looks like I'm just in time." He tossed me a glance, a question in his eyes. Was I going to be kind or did I still hold a grudge?

"Could I talk to you outside?" I reached for my coat and headed out the back door, knowing he would follow.

"I'm sorry—"

"I hope you under—"

We both spoke at the same time.

Matt grinned. "May I speak first?"

I nodded.

"I didn't know what else to do." A shadow passed over his eyes. "You're in danger, again, and it terrifies me."

"I'm sorry I acted like a child." I cupped his cheek. "But, I'm a strong-headed person. I love the mountain, but hate being forced into exile. I didn't ask for this. I planned on staying out of Daisy's murder, but then I got that warning without doing a thing. I can't sit back and wonder what's going on, what clues you've found out, etc. Norma is afraid for her life, Angela feels responsible for Daisy's death. I can't sit back and do nothing. They're counting on me."

He closed his eyes and leaned into my touch. "I know. No promises, but I'll try not to react so strongly."

"That's all I can ask." I wrapped my arms around his neck and pulled his face close for a kiss.

Matt's kisses increased in strength. He pulled me as close as was physically possible until my heart pounded. For a few minutes I forgot the world around us, the danger in the city, and the fact we weren't alone. Until Mom knocked on the kitchen window.

"Knock it off. We have work to do."

I sighed and rested my forehead on Matt's chest while I struggled to regulate my breathing. A heavy make out session was long overdue. Finding the privacy for one was next to impossible.

He groaned and took my hand, leading me into the cabin where we were greeted by wolf calls and laughter. Matt grinned and pulled out my chair. "Let's hear what you've all come up with."

"Great." Mom plopped a pad of paper on the table and handed me a sharpened pencil. "Let's make a list."

Angela eyeballed Matt, clearly not wanting him to know she had snooped around the police department. "I got nothing. Kids?"

Dakota folded his arms behind his head and leaned back in his chair. "Did you know the library is full of information?"

"Yes, as a matter of fact." I met Mom's amused glance.

"Well," he motioned his head toward Cherokee. "we discovered that the gang leader is named Stinger. There is a lot of mystery surrounding this man, and he is one bad cookie. You don't leave his gang alive, and betraying him results in some very bad stuff."

I shuddered, thinking of Jamal. "If Daisy had crossed him, that would explain her murder."

Matt's eyes widened. "You're investigating Stinger? Are you crazy?" He ran his hands through his hair. "You're asking to be shot. Every one of you. Is this the man that Norma thinks is after her?" He glanced at me. "When was the last time you spoke with her?"

"Before we came up here." My blood ran cold and I reached for my cell phone, dialing her number. After several seconds, I left a voice mail for her to call me. "Do you think she's missing?"

"I don't know. I'll check with her son tomorrow." Matt shook his head. "This is way over your head, Stormi."

"I agree, but I'm at a loss as to what to do. Jamal knows I'm asking questions. He warned me before I even asked them."

Matt pinched the bridge of his nose. "You're killing me."

"Okay." Mom tapped her pencil on the paper. "We know this is dangerous, we need to get a hold of Norma. Anything else? What about a list of suspects?"

"Stinger doesn't get his hands dirty," Matt said. "He would have had someone else kill Daisy, if that's what happened."

"Any more information on the poison ivy?" Mom really got into the sleuthing thing.

"It had been liquefied, a large amount, and stirred into the cream." Matt jumped to his feet and headed for the coffee pot. "The actual murderer has to have been at the party."

"I've got some info on that." I raised my hand and got strange looks from my family.

"We aren't in school, Aunt Stormi." Cherokee rolled her eyes.

"Right. Well, when I was locked up, and during my short acting stint, I found out that Ivy has access to a greenhouse, Lacey likes making hybrids of flowers, and Ginger wants to be a florist someday. Any one of those three could have killed Daisy.”

“And,” Greta spoke up, “someone on the outside could have given the ivy to Sissy. All those girls are suspects in my book.”

“This is nothing new.” We were getting nowhere. “Oh! I just remembered, someone told me that Ivy was the gang leader’s woman. Does that mean she’s dating Stinger?”

“Gang members don’t date,” Greta said. “They’re just together.”

“Whatever, the details don’t matter. Put Ivy at the top of the list.”

“Do you really think that Stinger would sacrifice his girlfriend?” Mom tilted her head. “Wouldn’t they have someone lower down the totem pole do the deed?”

“Can you all hear yourselves?” Matt turned, coffee mug in his hand. “Stop nosing around.”

We continued as if he hadn’t spoken. What was he going to do? Arrest everyone at the table? I drummed my fingers on the stained pine top. “Did anyone think to check past news reports to see whether anyone had died recently? Other than Daisy? Maybe she witnessed the murder and said too much.”

“I did,” Cherokee said. “Two young gang members were killed, execution style, over a month ago. Maybe Daisy saw that.”

Matt groaned.

“That’s it, isn’t it?” I pointed at him. “We’ve hit the nail on the head.”

“You know I can’t discuss the investigation.”

I grinned. “You don’t have to.” I turned back to the others. “So, what do we do now?”

“I can’t listen to this.” Matt took his coffee to the front porch.

“First, we need to make sure Norma is okay,” I said. “I’ll

try to meet her for coffee tomorrow." I tried Norma's number again. Still no answer. I was starting to get worried. She'd worked so hard to leave the lifestyle of a prostitute behind. What a horrible thing to end it all by being murdered. I couldn't let that happen.

"Greta, you were a police officer," I said. "What would you do next?"

"Try to protect the ones involved, which we've done by coming up here." She stared at the ceiling. "Then, we'd ask questions of potential witnesses, which we did this morning, then we'd sit around and discuss our findings. Really, not much different from what we're doing here. We could make a case board. It wouldn't be hard to find our suspects photos online. I'm sure they've all been arrested at least once."

"Good idea." I rummaged through the kitchen drawers for index cards. The wall next to the refrigerator would make a good board. "Dakota, take down that painting of the deer. We need that wall." Index cards in hand, I returned to the table.

"I'll go print off the photos." Greta pushed to her feet. "This could help Matt, too. We might see something he's missed."

Half an hour later, the wall was covered with photos and cards marked up with a marker. Matt opened the front door, took one look, and withdrew back outside. Poor guy. I'd have to go check on him in a few minutes.

I stared at the chaos on the wall. We'd placed the victim in the top left hand corner with a card under it that said "witnessed murder". Then, we had the suspects and why they were placed in the category. "We really need to get into Ivy's greenhouse."

"We have to find out where her mother lives first," Greta said. "I'm pretty sure that's where it is. She peered closer at the board. "Ivy's real name is Micayla Smith. The only address I could find was the one where she lives now.”

“We’ll have to follow her for a few days.” Hopefully, she spent time each day after her “shift” to play with her plants. “What time does the street close for business?”

Greta shrugged. “I think the girls work in shifts. So far, we’ve seen Ivy during the day.”

“Right. A girl in the jail said Ivy is more like a watchdog.”

“Then she probably doesn’t have regular hours.” Greta crossed her arms and stared at the board. “Angela, you can find out where she lives.”

“No, way. I’m with Matt on this one. I’m staying out of it from now on.” She crossed her arms. “I’m not going to jeopardize my job by snooping.”

“I thought you were going to get rich from your facial products,” Mom said.

“Like that’s going to happen now. I can’t get a single person to even take a sample.” She hung her head. “That endeavor was over as soon as it started.”

My heart went out to her, but eventually people would realize it wasn’t the product that had killed Daisy. “This is another reason to solve this case; so people aren’t scared of Angela.”

“I never said they were scared! Just wary.”

“Same thing.” I waved my hand.

“This is so unfair.” She glared. “You’re going to write a book about all this, make a ton of money, get your name in the paper, and I’ll be stuck barely making enough to survive on.”

“I know how you can get in the paper.” I smirked. “Get caught snooping at work and arrested. You’ll be famous.”

“Oh, you’d like that, wouldn’t you?”

“Girls.” Mom gave us the tone that told us to stop our bickering immediately. Even at almost thirty years old, I listened when she spoke in that way.

"Are you crazy people done yet?" Matt called from the door.

"Why aren't you in here helping?" Mom asked.

"I could get in a lot of trouble if I got involved with your shenanigans." Still, the board seemed to draw him like a magnet. "Impressive." He stood with legs spread shoulder width apart and arms crossed and studied the board. "Until your discussion at the table, I didn't know which of the women had access to plants. At least not to the degree it would have taken to kill Daisy. I hate to admit it, but that does help the investigation. The young man in your car was Denzel Peters, Daisy's main squeeze."

Interesting. He had obviously been privy to the same information that got her killed. "Does that mean we can keep doing what we're doing?" I put my arms around his waist and laid my cheek against his back.

"I wish you wouldn't, but short of actually arresting you, I won't be able to stop you." He put his hands over mine. "I'll keep being afraid of losing you."

Ouch. His words hurt. I tried not to get involved, for both our sakes, I really did. But now that it has been taken out of my hands, I'm glad he understands. This is me. The nosy neighbor of Oak Meadow Estates.

My cell phone rang, pulling me reluctantly, back to the table. Caller ID said it was Norma. "I've been so worried about you."

"I can't really talk." Her words barely carried through the phone. "Things are getting bad here. I've sent Tyler way. Can you meet me tomorrow? At the park. Nine o'clock?"

"Yes, but—"

"I have to go. I'm being watched. Look for the woman with the brown head scarf." Click.

I told the others of our conversation.

"I'll be there, out of sight," Matt said, holding up a hand at my protests. "That's the only way you're going."

I nodded. I'd feel a lot safer knowing he was there. "Maybe you could bring Koontz, too. The more the merrier when danger is involved."

14

Matt spent the night in a sleeping bag on the floor next to Dakota.

The next morning, my red hair disguised under one of my nephew's beanies, and wearing sweats, I rode with Matt to the park. We pulled into a parking slot and stared through the trees and empty benches. Not many people seemed to want to visit the park with sleet drizzling from the sky. I shivered and opened my door. "Wish me luck."

He grabbed my arm and pulled me close for a kiss. After leaving me dizzy, he said, "Good luck. There's Koontz. We'll be watching you."

I waved at Ryan, who had pulled alongside Matt's car, and took a deep breath of the freezing air. It was now or never. The closing of the car door sounded abnormally loud in the frigid morning. Hunched over against the cold, I headed for the center of the park.

The large fountain, turned off for the winter, took up precedence. Stone benches surrounded the impressive decorative feature. There was no sight of Norma.

I took a seat on one of the benches and glanced at my watch. Ten minutes after nine. I looked over my shoulder toward the parking lot, now hidden by a stand of fir trees. I didn't need to see Matt to know he was there. He would never leave me alone.

A black man in baggy jeans and tee shirt, a hat pulled low over his eyes, strolled past the bench. He didn't look my way, but I knew he'd seen me. The hair on the back of my neck prickled. I directed my gaze to the other side of the fountain. Two young men lounged against trees. I needed to go. Norma wasn't coming, and I was being watched by more than Matt and Koontz.

My cell phone beeped, signaling a text. I checked it. Norma had told me the meeting was compromised. I shoved my phone into my pocket and sprinted toward the parking lot.

"Get down!" Matt stepped from the trees, his gun drawn.

I'd no sooner hit the ground than gunfire exploded around me.

Koontz joined Matt, both taking refuge behind the fountain. I army crawled to the safety of the trees and watched in stunned horror as gang members fell. Where was the man I had seen first? I dashed for Matt's car, thankful he had left it unlocked, then locked myself inside. *Please, God, don't let him be killed.*

I scooted onto the floorboard and peered over the dashboard, ready to race back to Matt's side as soon as the shooting stopped. While I hid, three other cop cars, sirens screaming, sped into the parking lot.

One glanced through the window. "Stay there, ma'am." He sprinted away.

The shooting seemed to go on forever. When it did stop, I eased open the car door. Still not hearing any gunshots, I headed back in the direction of the fountain as an ambulance parked behind Matt's car.

I stepped into the aftermath of a war zone. While Matt and Ryan seemed to be unscathed, three young boys lay in pools of blood on the sidewalk. I recognized one of them as Jamal and rushed to his side, sidestepping Matt's outstretched arm.

I knelt beside the boy, and sighed. "What were you thinking?"

"This is part of the job." A smear of blood appeared in the corner of his mouth. "You shouldn't be here, Miss Stormi. You'll get me killed."

"He's right." Matt took me by the arm and pulled me to my feet. "You can speak to him later. Right now, these boys needs medical attention." He was all business, directing the other officers, keeping back the spectators that seemed to have appeared from nowhere, and ignoring me.

Happy he wasn't harmed, I was more than glad to wait in the car. I closed the door against the cold and did my best not to fidget. The man I had seen pass me while I waited for Norma, stared at me from the other side of Ryan's car. Although I'd never seen the man, instinct told me I looked into the shark eyes of Stinger. His look wasn't friendly.

When Matt appeared through the trees, Stinger melted out of sight, taking refuge in a thick stand of pine. I ran to Matt's side and threw my arms around him. Closing my eyes, I rested my face against his chest. "I think I just saw Stinger."

"What?" He held me at arm's length.

"He was watching me from over there and disappeared when you showed up. He's creepy."

"Wait in the car." Weapon in hand, Matt sprinted away.

I waited another fifteen minutes. When Matt returned, I threw myself back into his arms, not ever wanting to let go. "You're really okay."

He leaned his chin on the top of my head. "I'm fine. It was a setup."

"Not by Norma. She sent me a text warning me to stay away. It came through late." I didn't want to ever let him go.

"I need to talk to your friend, Jamal. Let's head to the hospital."

"Can I see him, please?" I gave him my most imploring

look. "I've been trying to befriend him for weeks, and he has been the one warning me to stay away."

"After I've questioned him, you can have five minutes." He tapped his finger on my nose. "No more."

I nodded. I didn't know why the young man mattered so much to me. Maybe it was because he was close in age to Dakota, and the thought of Dakota living such a dangerous lifestyle made me nauseous. If I could save one boy from the gang life, I'd feel as if I'd accomplished something priceless.

Writing books was fulfilling, and people had commented on how much the books helped them forget the bad in their own lives, and while that was pretty awesome, it wasn't saving a life. I wouldn't give up on Jamal just yet.

Another ambulance joined the first and I watched as the three boys were loaded into the backs. Another ten minutes, and Matt joined me in the car. We roared down the road toward the hospital.

"Are you sure you're all right?" I asked Matt.

A muscle ticked in is right jaw. "I had gunfights with kids. It's so senseless." He reached over and grabbed my hand. "But, yes, I'm uninjured. I'm sorry you had to witness that part of my job."

It did help me understand how he felt when I was in harm's way. I vowed to try my best to stay out of dangerous situations. Hopefully, the situations would find a way to leave me alone.

We pulled into the Emergency Room parking lot. Matt rushed me inside, his hand on the small of my back, and then gestured me toward the vinyl padded chairs. I chose one well away from the window. Matt followed the paramedics through a set of swinging doors.

I had my gun and tazer in my purse, but I was a bad shot and the tazer wouldn't do me any good unless an assailant got close. I never wanted to be close to Stinger again. I shuddered. I'd heard and written about lifeless eyes, but until then had never witnessed it personally. The man was evil and needed to be put away.

I texted Norma, asking her what happened and for her to contact me. I wouldn't rest easy until I knew whether she was okay.

How had our meeting been compromised? Unless someone knew of our phone conversation, there was no way of knowing about the planned meeting. Someone was watching Norma, and were way too close for comfort.

My phone dinged with an unknown number. It was Norma. She'd changed phones and told me to meet her in the hospital ladies' room. Glancing around to make sure Matt didn't need me, I followed the signs and pushed open the door.

Norma, looking more like a bag lady than her usual gorgeous self, grabbed me in a hug. "I heard about the shooting. Didn't you get my message?"

"Not in time." I returned her hug. "What happened?"

"I don't know. There were rumors about the gang meeting at the park, and I knew it wouldn't be safe for us there. Sormi, they're gunning for you."

"I figured that out for myself. Why? I don't know anything. Not really." I leaned against the sink. "Do you know where Ivy's mother lives?"

"In your neighborhood, on the street behind you. It's a yellow house with green shutters."

I knew the one. I'd passed it many times on my neighborhood patrol. "You need to take Tyler to the police and ask for protection. Have them get you out of here until things die down."

"I will. I'm meeting Tyler at the station in thirty minutes." She hugged me again. "Be careful." With those words, she left me.

I stepped out to the sight of Matt pacing the hall. "Where were you?"

"Meeting with Norma in the restroom. She's on the way to the police station to ask for protection."

He nodded. "Jamal will see you. We're putting him into protective custody as soon as the doctor's are finished. He'll be fine. The bullet just grazed him. He's a brave young man."

Grinning, I followed Matt to the boy's room. "Jamal."

"You don't listen very well, do you, Miss Stormi?" He smiled.

"No, I don't."

"I've told the cops all I know in exchange for getting me and my mom out of here. I've been undercover for months now. It's time for me to go. You need to leave, too."

"This is my home." I slipped my hand into his. "Who is Stinger?"

Matt hugged me from behind.

"No one knows. All I do know is that he's closer than you think. Word on the street is that he's on the cop payroll."

I glanced at Matt. His face seemed set in stone. "Norma is on her way there."

"We've got to go." He pulled me away from the bed.

"Take care, Jamal. I'll be praying for you."

Matt phoned Ryan and told him what Jamal had said. Taking my hand in his, we raced to his car. I prayed we wouldn't be too late.

"What did he mean on the payroll?" I asked, clicking my seatbelt into place. "Stinger is a cop?"

"We have a new guy on the force. Started six months ago. Drives a fancy car and wears expensive clothes. I should have known." He pounded the steering wheel. "Contact Norma and tell her to talk to no one but Koontz. He'll meet her next door at the diner."

I texted Norma while Matt called his partner. With my heart in my throat, we sped downtown in time to see Norma and Tyler entering the diner. Minutes later, Ryan escorted them out and put them in his car.

"Where is he taking them?" I wiped the fog from our breathing off the window in order to see better.

"To a safe house."

Koontz opened the two passenger side doors, and helped Norma and Tyler inside, before heading around to the driver's side. A shot rang out. He spun and fell.

Norma climbed over the seat and opened the driver's side door. Seconds later, she straightened and started the car.

Matt thrust open his door, gun in hand.

Norma gunned the car and pealed rubber out of the parking lot.

Matt dropped to his knees beside his partner and fired a shot between the two buildings. By now, officers swarmed the parking lot.

The radio in Matt's car crackled. I picked it up and pressed the bottom. After all, I'd seen it done on television. "Officer down. Shots fired. Send ambulance to the police department."

I replaced the radio in its holder and burst into tears.

15

For the second time that day, Matt and I were at the hospital, this time because of a dear friend. While I didn't fault Norma for taking advantage of Ryan's car, I'm not sure I could have driven off and let him lying there.

My heart ached for my friend lying on the operating table. I folded my arms across my stomach and rocked.

"Here. I thought you might like some coffee." Matt handed me a Styrofoam cup and sat in the seat beside me.

"Did the doctor say how long the surgery would last?" I breathed deep of the full-roasted aroma. My nerves already twanged so sharply, I wasn't sure coffee was a good idea. But it gave my hands something to do.

"A couple of hours."

A police officer stormed through the hospital doors and made a beeline toward us. My eyes traveled from his muddy shoes to his crisp uniform. "I'm Officer Reed," he said. "I've been assigned to guard the room of Ryan Koontz."

Matt shook his hand. "You're the new officer."

Reed nodded, his sharp dark-eyed gaze landing on me. "You must be the nosy woman we've all heard about."

"That would be me," I muttered. "But not by choice."

"Where did you transfer from?" Matt asked.

"Little Rock. I know Koontz from way back." He sat on the chair next to Matt.

I must have fallen asleep, because the next thing I knew, I woke with my head on Matt's shoulder and the doctor standing in front of us.

"Officer Koontz made it out of surgery just fine," the doctor said. "You'll be able to see him soon. The bullet passed through his ribcage, missing his heart. We dug out some bone fragments, but no major organs were damaged."

Praise God. My tears started anew.

Matt wrapped his arms around me, rubbing my back. "Thank you, doctor. Let us know when we can go back to see him."

"I'll send a nurse for you." The doctor gave us a nod, and headed down the hall, his soft-soled shoes squeaking with every other step.

"I want you wearing your bullet-proof vest every day," I told Matt, entwining my fingers with his. "You can even sleep in it." I couldn't get the picture of Ryan's body, bleeding, on the asphalt. If that had been Matt, I didn't know what I would have done.

"What about you? It could just as easily have been you standing next to Koontz." He lifted our hands and kissed the back of mine.

It was more imperative than ever that we find Daisy's killer and stop the gang from ruining our town. A year ago, stories of gang activity were only heard on the news and took place far away. Now, the danger was literally roaming our once peaceful streets.

My stomach growled loud enough to send Matt to the vending machine for a bag of chips and a soda for each of us. Reed declined, saying he had eaten right before hearing of Ryan's shooting.

A red flush showed under the man's dark skin, and he looked as if he was gritting his teeth. Anger showed in every line of his body. He and Ryan must have been very close. I knew Matt was upset, after all he was Ryan's partner, but Reed looked ready to explode. His demeanor scared me, to be honest. Not to mention that he looked familiar. I shrugged, not wanting to waste time on trying to figure out where I might have seen him before. Oak Meadows wasn't that big. We'd probably crossed paths at the grocery store or coffee shop.

By the time I'd finished my "lunch", the nurse arrived to take the three of us back to Ryan's room. Reed waited outside the door while Matt and I entered.

Ryan was groggy from drugs, but awake. "Hey."

"How are you?" Matt put a hand on his partner's arm. "You gave us quite a scare."

"The bullet wasn't intended for me. I think the target was Norma."

"We have Officer Reed on guard outside the door, just in case you were the target," Matt sat in a chair next to the bed, motioning for me to sit in the one on the other side.

I planted a soft kiss on Ryan's cheek before sitting.

"Close the door. There is something I need to tell you."

As Matt moved to close the door, Reed entered. "The nurse said time is up." He glanced unsmiling at Ryan. "You'll need to come back during normal visiting hours tomorrow."

"Not if it's part of the investigation." Matt squared his shoulders. "But we'll go. You get some rest, partner." He patted Ryan's shoulder, glared at Reed, and led the way out of the room.

"What's wrong?" I had to almost jog to keep up with Matt's rushed pace.

"I don't like the way Reed muscled his way in. He knows very well that I can visit anytime I want as part of the investigation."

"Then why did you let him make you leave?"

"Koontz could barely keep his eyes open. I'll come back tomorrow."

"Are we headed back to the cabin?"

"Yes. I want to use your laptop."

We hurried to his car and within minutes were speeding up the mountain. Something about Reed had set Matt off. While he usually had a lead foot, he rarely exceeded the speed limit more than eight miles over the limit.

"Slow down. This road is too curvy to go so fast." I gripped the strap over the door as if my life depended on it.

"Sorry." He slowed down.

"What's on your mind?"

"I can't talk about it yet. I need to do some research."

We drove the rest of the way in silence. When we pulled in front of the cabin, the family raced out to meet us.

"Mom said Mr. Koontz had been shot," Dakota said, the moment we stepped from the car. "Is he dead?"

"He's alive." Matt put his arm around my nephew. "Get in the house."

Cherokee, her eyes wide, stood on the porch. "We're supposed to go back to school on Monday. We can't go home. Not if people are shooting people."

I agreed that I didn't want my family in Oak Meadows. "Maybe your mother can excuse you for a family emergency."

"Why is Mom still working?" Tears shimmered in her eyes. "She's right in the middle of things."

"The police station is the safest place right now," Matt said, ushering us into the cabin.

"Really?" Cherokee crossed her arms. "Wasn't Mr. Koontz shot right in front of the police station?"

"The girl has a point," Greta said. "I hope that big teddy bear of a man is going to be okay."

"He'll be fine." Matt turned to me. "Stormi, may I borrow

your laptop."

I rushed to get it from my bedroom and handed it to him. He sat at the kitchen table and typed away on the keyboard.

"The new officer in town is guarding Ryan's room," I said. "In case he was targeted. Norma got away in Ryan's car." I plopped onto a chair and buried my head in my hands. "This is all so confusing and dangerous. I'm going to head home. The rest of you can stay here. The gang wants me, not the rest of you."

"Absolutely not." Matt peered at me over the top of the laptop.

"You and Greta can come with me." Although, I hated involving either of them. "It's only a matter of time until those chasing me follow us here. We're too secluded here."

Matt sighed. "Agreed. We'll head back to town and have around the clock protection. I've been looking into a security guard company and we can hire bodyguards."

"The neighborhood watch can keep an eye out, too," Mom said. "Nothing goes on in our neighborhood without everyone knowing about it. Let's get packed up! Don't forget the case board. We can use the dining room wall at home. I'll take all the photos down."

I really hated the fact they were all coming with me. The cabin had sounded like such a good idea at first, but now…the gang's reach was long. We were no safer here than in town. The security company sounded like a marvelous idea.

I headed to my room to pack the few things I had brought with me. Somewhere during the day, I'd lost Dakota's beanie. I could always buy him another. Tossing the rest of my things in my suitcase, I went to the kitchen to start taking down the case board on the wall.

Something about the day nagged at me. A valuable clue hovered on the edges of my mind. I was tired. Maybe a good night's rest or two would help me see things more clearly.

An hour later, vehicles loaded, and Sadie slobbering all over the back seat of Mom's van, we all set off down the mountain and back toward home. Angela had agreed to meet us there after work, leaving her packing to her daughter. It was as well. I loved my sister, but I wasn't in the mood to listen to any complaints. The day had been stressful enough.

The sound of a lawnmower came from the backyard when I climbed out of Matt's car. With a smile on my face for the first time that day, I dashed around the corner of the house. "Rusty!" I threw my arms around the simple-minded man that had disappeared months ago.

He stiffened under my embrace. "You haven't taken care of your yard."

"I was waiting for you." I held him at arm's length. "Where have you been?"

"Away. I'm home now."

"Across the street?"

He nodded. "Mother is gone. She was bad."

"She was sick, Rusty. Remember that."

"I like the little people."

"Yes, the new neighbors are very nice." My heart leaped to know he had returned. I'd worried about him so much the last few months.

"I have work to do." He turned back to mowing, dismissing me.

I headed to the front of the house. "Guess who is back."

Mom smiled. "How nice. We'll have to make sure the poor boy eats each day." She disarmed the alarm on the house and opened the door wide.

Ebony and Ivory dashed from their hiding places, meowing and winding around my legs. I scooped them both into my arms, thankful Angela had stopped by after work each day to check on them. Sadie dashed into the house and out the back door, barking at the lawn mower.

Rusty cried out in alarm. "No, dog!"

I laughed and rushed to save my gardener. Things were back to normal, at least for a little while.

Matt helped unload the suitcases and boxes of food. "I have some things I need to check on," he said, cupping my face. "Don't go anywhere."

"I wish you would tell me what is bothering you."

"I need to visit Koontz again before saying anything. Promise me you'll stay in the house. Your security detail will be parked out front in a dark SUV. Leave them alone."

"I promise."

He kissed me and rushed out the door.

"That man knows something that could help us crack this case." Greta stared after him, hands on her ample hips. "We need to have a deeper discussion about what went on today. Maybe I can figure out what he knows. Tell me about this new police officer."

"Reed? He knew Ryan a long time ago. That's all I know."

"Did you see anyone during any of the shootouts today?"

I froze. How could I have forgotten? "I think I saw Stinger."

16

"Tell me what you saw?" Greta said, grabbing an index card.

"He was tall, thin, black, and wearing baggy clothes." I shuddered, remembering the dead look in his eyes. "He stared at me over the car."

"Are you sure it was him?"

"How do I know? I've never seen Stinger."

"It could have been one of his main goons." Greta tapped a pen against the index card. "We really need to know what the man looks like."

"I'm not going around Melrose Street asking, if that's what you're hinting at." I opened the fridge and stared inside, looking for but not seeing, something to drink.

After the horrible day, my brain was tired and my body on the verge of exhaustion. I didn't want to discuss, or think about, the case, the gang, or shooting. "I'm going to bed. Maybe I'll see something with fresh eyes in the morning."

After a fitful sleep where I heard gunshots all night, and ran down a dark street away from a gang of over one hundred young men who all looked like the guy at the shooting, I splashed cold water on my gritty eyes. Instead of trying to fill the sleepless hours in my bed, I'd spent them in front of my laptop adding words to my current work-in-progress. The novel was coming along, slowly. Much like the murder case

I found myself involved in. I shook my head at the tired woman in the mirror, then stumbled to the kitchen to make coffee.

While the coffee brewed, I worked on putting our case board on the wall, hoping, praying, something would come to mind that would crack the case wide open and put an end to the terror. When I'd finished, I poured myself a mug of java and stepped back to take in the wall at one glance. Nothing popped out at me.

I caught movement out of the corner of my eye. Someone peered through the slit in the kitchen curtains. I screamed, dropping my cup. Hot coffee splashed up my leg. "Rusty!" I hopped over and yanked open the front door. "What have I told you about peeking through windows?" I left the door open and hobbled to the sink to put a cold rag on my stinging skin.

He stood in the open doorway, his head down. "I'm going to trim the bushes in the backyard. I didn't want you to be scared."

"Well, that didn't happen." I didn't want to be mean to him, he didn't mean any harm, but he really needed to stop being a Peeping Tom. "I've told you before that people don't like you staring at them."

"I see things."

I sighed. "Yes, we've been over this before. Wait." I glared at him. "What have you seen lately?"

He shrugged.

"Rusty."

"You are being watched." He turned and dashed across the yard.

I slammed the door closed and raced to the front window. The dark SUV Matt had told us would be out front was. Mrs. Olsen, also named Norma, watered her flowers, occasionally spraying the vehicle parked in front of her house. I would need to tell the security guys to move before she complained. The Salazars, our "little" neighbors walked a standard size poodle down the sidewalk. I smiled. The dog was as tall as they were. Mark Wood, the neighbor on the other side, glared at the Salazars as they strolled by. Their silly feud didn't seem to be over. Other than the neighbors, no one seemed to be paying any attention to my house. I would need to question Rusty further.

"Good morning." Greta breezed into the kitchen and straight to the coffee pot. "I laid awake last night thinking. I'm pretty sure the man you saw wasn't Stinger. Why would he reveal himself to you? I mean, he's been so careful up to now. Showing his face to you would put him at great risk of discovery."

I nodded. "We still don't know anything new." I grabbed a rag and knelt on the floor to clean up the shattered mug and spilled coffee. "I don't have a clue where to go from here."

"Just keep your eyes and ears open," she said, sitting at the table and staring at the photos and notes on the wall. "Something will pop out. Where do you suppose Matt went last night?"

"If I guessed, I would have to say he went to the hospital to talk to Ryan."

"Maybe we should do that very thing. He's a good friend of yours, right?"

"Yes." I narrowed my eyes. "You're trying to get me in trouble again."

"What's wrong with visiting an injured friend?" She grinned. "We can take him some treats from the shop. They're going to go bad if someone doesn't eat them."

"Isn't Mom going to return to work now that we're back?"

She shrugged. "We haven't talked about it. I suppose it would be okay if I went with her and you stayed locked in your house so I didn't have to worry about you."

I stood and tossed the shards into the garbage. "It isn't your job to worry about me."

"According to Matt it is."

"Well, you can stop now." I picked up the coffee-stained rag and threw it in the sink. "I appreciate your concern, I really do, but Mom will need you at the shop more. Besides," I motioned my head toward the sound of a hedge-trimmer coming from the backyard. "That man sees more than any private investigator. He'll call out an alert if anyone is around."

"That poor man isn't always around." Greta shook her head. "I'm having way too much fun living the good old days to stop now."

"I thought you worked a desk when you were an officer."

"I did, but I heard things and learned a lot."

"Fine. We'll go see Ryan, but tomorrow, you're back to working with mom." Who was I to deny a fellow snoop? "Give me fifteen minutes to get dressed." I dashed upstairs to my room and threw on a pair of jeans and a long-sleeved tee shirt. "We're stopping for coffee," I yelled as I thundered down the stairs to disarm the alarm. "I spilled mine."

Greta joined me and we headed outside to the jeep. I backed out of the driveway as Mom stepped onto the porch, waving her arms for us to stop. No way was I letting her accompany us. She was in enough danger. I waved and roared down the street.

"That was mean." Greta buckled her seat belt.

"I don't want her involved any further."

We stopped at Heavenly Bakes and filled a box with bite-sized cakes. I sampled a few as I chose the assortment, squelching my complaining empty stomach.

At the hospital, I pulled into the parking spot closest to the door, which was still twenty cars away and cut the ignition. "Let me do the talking."

"Yes, boss." Greta climbed from the jeep. "Has anyone ever told you that you can spoil their fun faster than a meteor hitting a water park?"

"Not in so many words, no." I led the way into the hospital and pressed the button on the elevator. Some of the fear that hung over me the last few days dissipated. How much danger could we be in visiting someone at the hospital?

Reed wasn't at his post when we arrived at Ryan's room so Greta and I waltzed right in. Ryan was sitting up, staring morosely at at bowl of jello. "Tell me you brought me something other than baby food to eat."

"Hello to you, too." I planted a kiss on his cheek and set the box of cakes on the windowsill. "You can have those as soon as the doctor says it's okay."

"You're a heartless woman."

"I've been told that before." I grinned and sat in the chair next to the bed. "How are you feeling?"

"Fine, I guess, but I'm starving. Once I move my … uh … well, you know, they'll let me eat real food." He eyed the box of treats.

"When we were here the other day," I put a hand on his arm, "you said there was something you needed to tell us. What was it?"

"I'm not at liberty to say." He shoved his food tray away.

"Why not?"

"I was drugged up pretty good yesterday. Who knows what I was really going to say? Most likely, it was something that would get me in hot water." He glanced over my left shoulder, not meeting my eyes.

He was lying.

"If you know something that will stop all this—"

"I don't." He crossed his arms. "You should stop asking me. Since I can't help protect you, you're only increasing the danger. Where's my car?"

"Norma drove off in it."

"My gun is in that car." He shook his head. "I don't mind taking the bullet intended for her. I'm glad she got away."

"Do you know the identity of the person who ordered Norma killed?" I squeezed his arm. "Do you know who Stinger is?"

"What are you doing in here?" Reed stormed into the room. "No one comes in here without my permission."

"I'm visiting a friend. There's no rule against that." I released Ryan's arm and lifted my chin. "We're here during visiting hours." Since we had yet to stop for coffee, my mood was not one where someone could come at me aggressively and expect me to back down.

"I'm calling Detective Steele. You're refusing to follow my orders." Reed reached for his radio.

"No need." Greta stood. "We're leaving."

"Do I know you?" He asked.

"Nope." She rushed me from the room and into the elevator, repeatedly pushing the down button until the doors closed. Reed watched us from Ryan's doorway.

"What was that all about?" I jogged to keep up with her as she hurried to my jeep.

"Get in and I'll tell you."

We got in and locked the doors. "I'm listening."

"I've seen that man before, and he wasn't in uniform."

"Where?"

"Little Rock. He may be an officer, but he's something else, too. I think he's Stinger."

My heart dropped. "He's guarding Ryan." I reached for the door handle, intending to run in and rescue my friend.

"Which really makes me wonder." Greta pierced me with her stare. "Ryan is still alive, isn't he? If Reed is Stinger—"

"Then Ryan knows about it." I leaned my forehead against

the steering wheel. "I need to call Matt, and we need to visit Jamal." I dialed the hospital front desk for Jamal's room and was informed he had been released. "We're heading to Jamal's house. Get my gun out of the glove compartment."

"I thought you kept it in your purse." Greta retrieved it and set it in my lap.

"Normally, I do, but I stuck it in there on the drive back from the cabin."

I drove us to Jamal's house, sad to know that Norma wasn't home. She was in hiding, and hopefully still alive. I parked in Norma's driveway and after exiting the jeep, stuck my weapon in the waistband of my pants and pulled my shirt down to cover it. The usual group of young gang members was nowhere to be seen.

Glancing around us, we made our way to the Brown's front door. I knocked and stepped back.

Shaunda opened the door. "What do you want?"

"I'd like to speak with Jamal."

"He ain't here."

"Stop it, Momma. Let her in," Jamal called from inside.

We stepped into a room full of boxes and suitcases. "You're leaving?" I moved to stand in front of the sofa where Jamal lay.

"It's not safe here," Shaunda said. "I need to get my boy away while he's still breathing." She bopped him upside the head. "Him and his stupid choices."

"Ow!" Jamal put a hand to his head. "I told you I wanted out, but they wouldn't let me."

"They shot you!"

"I'm pretty sure it was the cops that shot me." He took a deep breath. "The police department is sending a moving truck for us in thirty minutes. They're placing us in protective custody. I bet you're here to talk about Stinger."

17

"That name is not allowed in my house." Shaunda sat on an overflowing suitcase in an attempt to close it.

"If you're running, why are you taking all of your things?" Greta asked. "Why not just go?"

"Not everyone has the money to replace belongings." Shaunda bounced and grunted, finally getting the case closed and latched. "These are our memories."

"What do you know about Stinger?" I turned my attention back to Jamal.

He plucked at a loose thread on the unraveling Afghan across his legs. "Rumor has it that he's a cop."

I choked back a gasp. Greta and I were on the right track. "Anything else?"

"He gives his assignments through text messages." Jamal dug a phone out of his pocket. "Here. The last thing I got was that our target was at the park. I wasn't happy to see it was you."

I glanced at the text. "I think the target was supposed to be Norma."

"I heard her and Tyler disappeared."

I nodded, not sure how much to tell him. Saying he wanted to change his lifestyle wasn't the same as doing. "Do you know where Ivy's greenhouse is?"

"Yeah, but I don't advise going there." He wrote an

address on the back of an empty envelope and handed it to me. "If her or Stinger finds out you went there and harassed her mom, they'll kill you."

"And us, if they find out he told you." Shaunda opened the front door. "Y'all need to leave before someone finds out you're here. My boy is still mending."

She was right. Greta and I needed to go. "Take care of yourself, Jamal. I hope you can leave this all behind you."

"Be careful, Miss Nelson. You're one of the good guys."

"Thank you. What are Ivy's hours?"

"Most of the time, she works during the day. She spends her nights with Stinger, messing with her plants in between."

I met Greta's gaze, knowing without saying what our next stop was going to be. I shook Jamal's hand, bending close enough to whisper for him to seek the Lord.

He nodded and told me to keep a close eye on Sissy. She wanted Ivy's spot in the chain of command.

I turned and thanked Shaunda, and left, knowing I would never see either one of them again. I sent a prayer heavenward for their safety, and returned to the jeep.

"Do you think they'll be all right?" I asked Greta.

"I think so. The boy seems to have his head on straight now. Better late than never. They can start over somewhere else."

I really needed my coffee, so we made a trip to the coffee shop. It seemed strange not to see Tyler behind the counter. The friendly aroma of brewing coffee and baking pastries helped relieve some of the tension.

"Stormi!"

The tightness in my muscles returned along with the shout from Sarah Thompson. She rushed toward me.

"I heard all about the shooting. Are you going to put it in your next book? I think I will, if that's all right. Can I interview you? It would be great to have a first hand accounting of it.”

I waited for her to take a breath. “A shooting in a romance novel?”

“Oh, yes.” She wiggled her eyebrows. “Something that traumatizing could very well send my hero and heroine straight into each others arms. It will be positively steamy.”

No doubt. Her erotic books left me feeling dirty just glancing at them.

The line moved forward and I ordered Greta and I the largest frozen mocha blend drinks they carried. All the while, Sarah rattled on about how exciting my life was and how I had so many experiences to write about. I’d gladly hand those experiences over to her.

“Where are you going?” She trotted after Greta and I. “Can I tag along? I could use the research.”

“Look.” Greta turned on her like a pit bull. “This isn’t a game. People are dying. Go back to your smut books and mind your own business.”

Sarah’s mouth opened and closed like a stranded fish. She blinked rapidly, then spun on her heel and marched back to her laptop.

“Well.” Greta exhaled sharply. “That worked as planned.”

I laughed. “And you call me mean.”

“There you are.” Mom accosted us the moment we stepped outside. “Why did you leave without me this morning? I’ve been looking everywhere for you.”

“It’s for your safety, Mom.” She waved away the offer of my drink.

“Tough. I’m coming with you now. Today is my last free day. I start back to work tomorrow.” She climbed into the front passenger seat of my jeep, not taking no for an answer.

“That leaves me the back seat.” Greta climbed in behind Mom.

Just call us the three stooges. I turned the key in the

ignition and drove to the opposite side of town, hoping, praying, no one was home at Ivy's mother's house.

A sign in front of the quaint cottage-style home advertised flowers for sell. If caught by someone other than Ivy, we had an out if caught. I drove down the block and parked. We could hoof it for a while. "Keep it quiet. We want to snoop undetected."

"That has never happened," Mom pointed out. "We need to practice sneaking around."

"Or just act as if you belong there," Greta said. "Don't act guilty, act outraged when accused, and continue on your way. Works every time."

I should have come alone. Their chatter would alert people two miles away. With a glance at the closed curtains over the house's windows, I headed around back. Sure enough, a greenhouse as large as the house took up the entire backyard.

My heart rate accelerated. We were finally getting close to finding out Ivy's role in Daisy's murder. "You two be quiet. We need to be able to hear if someone is coming."

I pushed open the glass door and stepped into the warmth and humidity of an Arkansas summer in July. Every color imaginable, both real and imaginary, greeted us. I could spend hours putting around such a place. The scent of dozens of rosebushes filled the air, seeming to suffocate the room with their sweetness. I told Mom to leave the door open and headed down one of the aisles.

Not being a stranger to poison ivy, I expected to see pots of the stuff growing in the aisles. I didn't spot a single plant. Another dead end. "We're wasting our time."

The others agreed after each of us had walked up and down the aisles several times. "I would've bet my mother's china cabinet that we'd find the stuff here that killed Daisy," Greta said. "What now?"

I shrugged.

The sound of car doors slamming, sent us dashing out the back door of the greenhouse. We hunkered down in the thick bushes surrounding the property.

"Mama left the doors open again," Ivy said. "She complains that it's too hot and is too stupid to understand that's what helps the flowers grow."

"Just show me what you have new."

"That's Ginger," I whispered.

Greta put a finger to her lips.

"If I'm going to open my own shop soon, I need to know that I have a supplier that can keep up with customer demand," Ginger said.

"You expect to be that successful, do you?" Ivy's sarcastic tone drifted through the open back door. "Who in their right mind will shop at a store owned by a former prostitute?"

"Anyone that doesn't know!"

"You're delusional. Shut up and look around. "I need to close these doors before the cold hurts my plants."

A branch tickled my lower back. I swatted it away, keeping my gaze locked firmly on Ivy.

"If I had known I'd be squatting in the bushes, I wouldn't have worn these pants," Greta said after the door closed. "They keep sliding down. They aren't made for crouching."

"Shhh." I wasn't taking any chances of being heard, even with the door closed. "Duck walk after me. We need to get to the front of the house. Then, we can question Ivy about looking at her flowers. If we take our time looking, maybe we'll see something we missed."

We practically crawled through the bushes until we were out of sight. I plucked a twig from Mom's hair and straightened my shirt. My palms itched, and I rubbed them down the leg of my jeans. "Ready?"

"As I'll ever be," Mom said.

Greta nodded.

I squared my shoulders, rubbed my hands down my legs again, and marched around the corner of the house. "Ivy." I pasted on a big smile and waved.

Her face registered shock a mere second before going blank. "How did you get here?"

"We drove. We had the address wrong and parked down the block, but then saw the sign," I explained. "We had no idea this was your place."

"It belongs to my mother."

Mom stepped forward. "We're wanting a weekly delivery of flowers to grace my bakery shop. Perhaps you're the very person who can help us."

Greta scratched her back and nodded. "May we see what you have to offer?"

"Come on." Ivy's tone lacked enthusiasm, but she led us to her flowers. "Some of the plants are seasonal. Why don't you look around, tell me what you like, and I'll surprise you each week."

"That sounds perfect." Mom grinned and pretended to study what she'd looked at only minutes before.

Ginger stood off to the side, a scowl on her overly made up face. "I'm going to have a florist shop soon. You could wait and order from me."

"Perhaps we will, dear," Mom said. "But we need to look around first."

My hands wouldn't stop itching. I rubbed them harder on my jeans. The skin where Greta's shirt hiked up was red from her scratching. I forced myself to admire the roses and daisies, when all I wanted to do was head home and take a shower.

Ivy stood by the door and watched with eyes as cold as Sadie's nose. I wasn't sure she believed our story of how we had come to be there, but without proof, couldn't prove I was lying. We were safe. For now.

Her phone rang, and she pulled it from her cleavage. Mom had always said God intended for the bosom to be used for more than feeding babies. Obviously, some people used theirs as a purse. I glanced at my small to middle sized bust and shrugged. I had enough to look okay in clothes. That was good enough for me.

"Well, I think I've seen everything." Mom held out her hand to Ivy.

Ivy propped the phone between her ear and her shoulder to return Mom's shake. "Hold on, sweetheart. I've some floral customers." She handed Mom a business card, a bit limp from sitting on a table in the greenhouse, and returned to her phone call.

The three of us hurried to the jeep before she got suspicious at our quick walk-through.

"I'm not sure we accomplished much," I said, starting the jeep. I put my red, itchy hands on the steering wheel and pulled away from the curb.

"I wouldn't say that." Mom grinned.

"Why not?"

"Because Greta has poison ivy on her back and your hands are covered with it." She clicked her seatbelt in place with a flourish. "I'd say we accomplished quite a bit."

"From the bushes?" I glanced at her. "It's too cold."

"There's a small pot of it sitting near the back door. We all brushed against it on our wild dash outside. I really have no idea how we missed it the first time around." She slapped the dashboard. "Get us home. We've found Daisy's killer."

18

"This isn't enough to arrest her," Matt said, looking at my hands. "But it does put her at the top of the suspect list."

"Daisy died from poison ivy, and Ivy is growing it. What more do you need?" I pulled my hands free and applied anti-itch cream to my palms.

"Solid evidence. We don't want the murderer to walk free because of a technicality."

"I guess my death will be evidence enough."

His face darkened. "No one told you to go snooping around Ivy's house or to go talk to Jamal. I am curious about Reed, though. There is something fishy about him."

"I knew that's why you took off. You think he's involved." A person heard about dirty cops all the time. "Can you request someone else to guard Ryan?"

"We don't have the manpower, and again, I don't have proof." He sat on the sofa next to me. "One good thing has come of all this, though. Gang activity has slowed down."

"They're probably waiting to see what I'll do next." I rested my head against the back of the sofa and tried not to rub my hands on my pants. The itching was going to drive me crazy.

"Here." Greta entered the living room and handed me an ice cube. "It helps a little."

"Thanks."

Mom carried in a tray with tea and cookies. "I still say you have enough to lock her up. What does the police department need? Another murder?"

"We're hoping Ivy will lead us to Stinger." Matt reached for a cookie.

"Good luck." Mom set the tray on the coffee table and sat in a wingback chair opposite Greta. "We haven't seen hide nor hair of that evil man."

"What do we do about Jamal's words about Sissy?" I plopped a chocolate-chip cookie in my mouth. "Maybe Ivy isn't the killer. It could be one of the other girls wanting Ivy out of the way. Just because Sissy doesn't talk about plants, doesn't mean she wouldn't know how to get them."

"Good point," Mom said. "Matt, does the department have a prostitute on their payroll?"

"Excuse me?"

"You know. A stool pigeon. Someone we can ask about the inner workings of … those people."

He shook his head. "I can't divulge that information."

"True." Mom tapped her finger against her lips. "That would endanger them."

"What about the undercover agents in the gang? Can they tell us anything?" I asked.

"How did you find out about that?" His brow furrowed. "Oh, never mind. I won't get a straight answer anyway. Keep that information to yourself, please. It's dangerous."

I nodded. "So, where do we go from here?"

"I'm heading back to work." He leaned over and kissed me. "Dinner tonight? Wear something sexy."

My face heated. We were way overdue for some alone time. "I'll be ready. Seven?"

"Sounds good." He kissed me again and left.

I sat on my hands and propped my feet on the table, only to get them slapped by my mother for being too close to the food. "Sorry. Any ideas on what to do next?"

"Someone needs to infiltrate the girls on Melrose." Mom gave a nod to emphasize her point.

"They all know me."

"I wasn't talking about you."

Ouch. That was a blow to my self-esteem. Didn't my mother think I had what it took in the looks department? "Then who?"

"I was thinking of Angela."

"Well, she does dress the part," I said. "But, I doubt she'll do it. It isn't like she can just set up shop under a street light." At least I didn't think so. I wish I knew more about the young girl I'd shared a cell with. Maybe she wouldn't be too hard to find.

"Greta, do you know how to get into the mugshots? I'd like to look someone up on the computer."

"Sure." She stuffed a cookie in her mouth. "It's easy."

I fetched my laptop and handed it to her. Soon, we were flipping through photos of girls picked up for prostitution. "There's so many. Check the ones in the last week."

Greta typed in a date.

"There she is." I pointed at the young blond girl. "She was picked up on Hunter Drive. That's one street over from Melrose, right? Anyone ready for another road trip?"

"Let me get my purse." Mom grabbed the tray and dashed to the kitchen.

"She probably won't tell you anything more than what she told you in jail."

"I need to pretend to be a customer." I bit my lip. "I'll dress in Dakota's clothes again. Then, when she gets in the van, we'll see what we can get from her within a few minutes. That ought to keep her safe." I was spending way too much time on the seedy side of town. "We'll have to hurry. I need to get ready for my date."

Half an hour later, I was pulling up to the curb where our

target slouched against a brick wall. "Hey." I deepened my voice and kept my head down, hoping the baseball cap I wore would cover enough of my face.

"Hey, yourself. Looking for a good time?"

"Hop in. I've got fifteen minutes."

She cocked her head, then obviously deciding I wasn't a crazy serial killer, opened the passenger side door. I crawled between the seats and joined Greta and my mother in the back. The girl did the same.

"What is this? I'm not into that … kind of stuff."

I whipped off my hat. "I'll give you fifty dollars to answer some questions."

"Oh, it's you." She relaxed. "Show me the money first."

I scooted between her and the door. I wasn't giving her the money *and* an opportunity to flee. I dug a wrinkled fifty dollar bill from the pocket of my jeans and handed it to her. "What's your name?"

"My street name is Starr. I'm not telling you my real name."

"Fair enough. What can you tell us about Sissy?"

"Has anyone ever told you that you are a very nosy person?" She stuffed the money in her bra.

"All the time." To which Mom and Greta nodded. I turned my face to ignore them.

"Sissy is ambitious," Starr said. "She wants the power that Ivy has. Until the gang came down from Little Rock, no one had ever heard of these gals."

"Did you follow the gang?"

She shook her head. "I'm independent. I came down from St. Louis. I had dreams of going to school, but that didn't pan out. So, here I am."

"You can always go home."

"Home is worse than what I have now. What else do you want to know?"

"Will you be willing to work for me? I'll pay you for information." And somehow, I'd figure out how to get this girl off the streets and into college. "We need to know who Stinger is and who killed Daisy. Anything will help us."

"I've seen Stinger."

I couldn't believe our fortune. "What does he look like?"

"Tall, thin, black. He has a tattoo of an upside down cross on his left upper arm." She glanced at the door. "My fifteen minutes is up. More time means more money."

I wrote my phone number on a slip of paper. "Call me if you discover anything else. How can I reach you?"

She gave me a sad smile. "You know where to find me." She opened the door and slipped out.

"That wasn't a total waste of time," I said, sliding back into the driver's seat. "We know that Stinger has a tattoo."

"Yep." Mom climbed into the passenger seat. "Now, all we have to do is find him and get him to take his shirt off."

"We could sneak into the gym at the station," Greta said. "We might see more than his tattoo though. Now, mind you, I'm going on the assumption that Reed is Stinger."

I nodded. We needed to know whether Reed had the tattoo. "I'll tell Matt."

There was no way I was going into a men's locker room or the gym. If I stepped into a gym, anyone watching would fall down in a fit of laughter. They just weren't places I frequented. I could always dump hot coffee on him to get him to remove his shirt. I grinned at the idea. One small act toward a potentially evil man. But what if he wasn't Stinger? I would have crossed the line of my past embarrassing moments to accept the award for the world's worst stunt.

Back at home, I took a hot shower and raided Angela's closet for something sexy, but that wouldn't allow me to freeze to death. How she kept from getting pneumonia with her barely there clothes was a true mystery.

"How many times have I said you need to go shopping?" Angela entered her room and tossed her purse on the bed.

"A million and one." I didn't have a need for a lot of nice things. The occasional conference and book signing, other than date nights with Matt, were the only times I needed to dress up.

"You have a nice body, Stormi. You need to dress it better."

"I haven't heard any complaints from Matt."

She shrugged and pushed me out of her closet. "Here. This will cover you up and cling to all the right places. Just don't rip it up like the last dress you borrowed."

"I was running from a killer. If it happens again, I'll strip to my underwear."

"Good idea. Your underwear would scare off anyone." She grinned, her gaze taking in the not very sexy bra and panties I was wearing, and perched on the side of her bed. "I heard something at work today that might interest you."

"Really?" I clutched the dress to my chest and faced her.

"The cops are regularly patrolling the streets where the gangs and prostitutes hang out. They're bringing in everyone they see for intense questioning, keeping most of them overnight, and then loading them into a van and taking them out of town."

"Can they do that?" What about Starr? If she were arrested, I'd lose my informant.

She shrugged. "I don't know if they can, but they are. Only those they know for sure belong to one of those two groups, though. Looks like the women from Norma's party won't be around for long."

"We might never find out who killed her."

"That isn't our business, Stormi." Her shoulders slumped. "I've thrown all my skin care products in the garbage. I'm doomed to be a receptionist for the rest of my life."

"There's nothing wrong with being a receptionist."

"I wanted more out of life. I wanted to marry a rich man. Instead, I got two children out of wedlock and still don't have a steady boyfriend. Why do you get all the luck?"

I didn't count myself as very lucky. I worked hard writing my books. If Angela wanted to trade luck, she could have mine. There wasn't anything lucky about having another psycho after me.

I didn't understand. I tried to be a good Christian girl, writing my books, and helping my family where I could. Instead, I ended up fighting for my life on a regular basis. It kind of sucked.

"Thanks for the dress. I'll try to take care of it."

Back in my room, I put on the long-sleeved dress. Angela was right. It clung to every part that needed to be clung to and swayed when I walked. I felt like a fiery temptress in with my red hair and black dress. A pair of red heels completed the outfit.

The doorbell rang. I grinned. I planned on kissing Matt thoroughly enough to knock both our shoes off. A night without fearing that someone followed me. A night secure in the affection of a handsome man. These were all I wanted.

Whether I got them or not was to be seen. Our last dinner date had ended in a bullet through a window.

19

Matt's eyes widened as I descended the stairs and he let out a whistle. "You clean up good, girl."

"You're not so bad yourself." He wore black slacks and a royal blue button up shirt that brought out the blue in his eyes. I was a lucky woman.

Slipping my arm in his, he led me to his car and opened the door for me to slide in. Since the dress fell to knee-length, I kept my modesty. It was a sign of a good evening ahead.

We parked in front of our favorite restaurant. Matt hurried to open my door, holding out his hand to help me from the car. Excitement at having some time alone with my man bubbled in me like carbonated soda. I linked my arm in his and pressed close to his side as we stepped inside the restaurant to muted lighting, the clink of eating utensils, and the smile of a waiting hostess.

"Follow me, please." She grabbed two menus and led us to a back corner with a window looking out on a fountain.

"I called ahead," Matt whispered, his breath tickling my neck. "Tonight, it's just us. No case, no gang, no family."

I couldn't agree more. I slid into my side of the booth and glanced out the window. Bushes surrounded the fountain, blocking the view of the street. A feeling of de ja vu swept over me. It wasn't the same window that a bullet had shattered months ago, but I still felt exposed. No, tonight was about Matt and me. I wouldn't let anything else cloud my mind.

"You look beautiful." Matt smiled over the top of his menu.

"Thank you." I wasn't good with compliments. I ducked my head and immersed myself in the large selection of dishes printed on the menu. While I had never considered myself unattractive, I didn't think I would ever get used to the fact that a man as handsome as Matt was interested in me. Especially with my tendency to get in trouble.

"What can I get for you two?" The waitress, dressed in black slacks and a white blouse with a bow tie, stopped at our table.

Matt raised at an eyebrow at me.

"I'll take the Salmon," I said.

Matt ordered the same.

I opened my mouth to tell him about Stinger's tattoo, but stopped before saying anything. I wasn't going to spoil the evening.

Matt reached across the table and took my hand in his. "Let's talk about us."

"As in?" *Please, don't say you took me out to dinner to break up with me.* I'd tried putting the brakes on our relationship not too long ago, only to find out at that time, that Matt wasn't in agreement. Had he changed his mind?

"Where are we going, Stormi? After a year, we need to discuss our future."

Uh-oh. This was serious.

"Stormi, I l—"

The waitress brought our salads, interrupting his use of the "L" word. While I felt the same, I had a phobia about being the first one to say it. Life hadn't been kind in the romance department.

Matt sighed and picked up his fork. "Maybe now isn't the time."

"It's the perfect time. What were you going to say?" I glued my gaze on his face, silently begging, pleading for him to finish his sentence.

The waitress arrived with our bread. "Oh, I forgot to take your drink order. What can I get you? I'm new and not very good at this I'm afraid."

"Tea for me," I said. I bit my tongue in order not to be rude, when all I wanted to do was tell her to stay away.

"Same." Matt smiled at me. "It will wait until there are less interruptions."

Great. I slumped back on the seat. I'd almost heard the words I longed to hear, only to have a bumbling waitress spoil it.

We talked about mundane things, tiptoeing around Daisy's murder and Ryan's shooting. By the time our main meal arrived, I was frustrated beyond measure. I set my fork on the side of my plate with a clatter. "This is ridiculous. I love you, Matt. You're the most important person in my life, despite my lack of showing it." I took a deep breath. "And Stinger has a tattoo." There. I felt cleansed.

He looked shocked for a moment, then gave me a smile that started with a crook on one corner of his mouth and spread to the other. "I'm not sure which statement to address first, but I'll go with I love you. You've made me a happy man."

"Is that what you were trying to say?"

"Yes." He took my hand again. "I've been wanting to for weeks, months. I love you, Stormi Nelson. Wanna be my one-and-only?"

I laughed. "I thought I was."

"Darlin', no other woman comes close."

"You love me despite the way I drive you crazy?"

"You make me crazy in more ways than one." He winked.

My face heated. "Stop it."

"I like it when your face turns red. It's cute."

I tossed my napkin at him, which he caught in mid-air, kissed, then tossed back at me. I wasn't quite as graceful. The napkin hit me on the nose.

At that moment, I almost wished I hadn't made a pledge in high school to wait for sex until marriage. So many people didn't, but I wasn't most people. I wanted to make sure, without a doubt, that a man loved me no matter what before I gave up what I could only give once. Matt had never pressured me, for which I was grateful. I gulped my ice tea before I made an indecent proposal to him and made a fool of myself.

"Now, about the tattoo. How do you know this?"

"Oh, I have my sources." I tried to act coy. From the way he looked at me, his features growing more stern, I had failed miserably. "When I was in jail," I stared back, "I made some very important friends. One of them happens to be a … you know. I'm paying her to be my informant. She told me."

His jaw dropped. "Since you're so determined to get involved in law enforcement, why didn't you become a cop instead of a writer."

I shrugged. "I thought writing books would be safer. How wrong I was."

"If you didn't get your picture in the paper every six months, you might have accomplished that goal." He shook his head. "I don't want to fight tonight. I want to talk about us."

"Don't you want to know who my informant is? Of course, she won't talk to anyone but me, but I thought you might be curious."

"I'm very curious." He tossed his napkin on his plate. "So, who is she?"

"Will you keep it a secret?"

He narrowed his eyes.

"Okay. She goes by the name Starr."

He couldn't have looked more surprised if I had announced I was really a man. "Seriously?"

"Yes, why?" There was definitely something he wasn't telling me.

"Short, blond, looks like she's sixteen?"

"Yes."

He stared out the window, a muscle ticking in his jaw. "I don't have a clue what to do about this," he muttered. "What does the tattoo look like?"

"An upside down cross." I figured I might as well tell him everything. "Rumor is that Reed is Stinger. Is there anyway you can see him with his shirt off? I thought about sneaking into the gym, but that really isn't my thing."

"You know too much." He transferred his attention back to me. "I'll find a way."

"Hurry. He's the one guarding Ryan's room."

"Yeah, there's something fishy about that."

"I thought so, too. Greta and I were thinking—"

"Stormi, please. Let me handle this. I appreciate the information you've dug up, but things are escalating. The police are cracking down hard on the gang and things are getting ugly."

"But, I'm helping you, and it keeps me from going crazy locked in my house."

"I really don't know why I waste my breath."

He looked so sad, tears burned my eyes.

"I'm being careful, and wearing a disguise every time I question someone."

"With your looks, a disguise isn't enough."

"Thank you, I think." I twisted my napkin.

"Greta, especially, should know better. She was an

officer."

"Behind a desk."

"Doesn't matter. She knows the rules." He raised his hand for the check.

I'd done it again. I'd ruined a wonderful evening by talking about things I had no business talking about. "Let's take a walk though the restaurant garden. I don't want the night to end."

"That's the second best thing you've said all night."

Minutes later, hand-in-hand, we strolled through crunchy dried leaves and evergreen trees. Matt pulled me into the bushes. "Let's celebrate saying I love you."

"That's the second best thing *you've* said all night." I wrapped my arms around his neck.

He pressed close. A tree trunk stopped us from going farther, the bark rough against my back. Matt lowered his head and nuzzled my neck. My breath hitched in my throat as his kisses deepened, moving to my lips.

"You're my heart, Stormi," he whispered, his breath hoarse against my lips.

I couldn't think of anything but the way his kisses felt, his strong body against mine, his hands caressing my back. I should've said no, but gave into the passion instead. All coherent thought fled my mind and I returned his kiss with all the passion pent up inside me.

When I could no longer breath, I pulled away and rested my forehead on his chest. His heart raced under my hand. My kisses seemed to affect him as strongly as his did me. It wasn't wise to spend too much time alone. While I knew we couldn't step over the line in a public place, passion tended to make people lose all reason.

"We should go," I said, my chest heaving.

"Yeah." He cupped my face, staring into my eyes, his glittering in the moonlight. "You make me lose my mind.

You're a fire-haired temptress, Stormi Nelson, casting a spell on me that I can't break."

"Do you want to break the spell?"

"God, no." He kissed me again, this time with a tenderness that brought tears to my eyes and down my cheeks. He rubbed them away with his thumbs. "Don't cry. Love is a wonderful thing. I'm blessed to have someone like you love me."

Voices coming down the path caused us to step apart. Matt took my hand in his. We strolled without speaking around a small man-made pond. I was content to walk in silence and soak in the beauty of my surroundings and the love of the man beside me. The night had been more than I'd hoped for. No bullets or shattering glass. No crazed maniac staring at us through the window. It was possible to have a date night without almost getting killed. The fact my borrowed dress was unharmed was an added bonus.

Matt pushed open a wrought iron gate and ushered me ahead of him. We rounded the corner of the restaurant.

"What in Hades name?" Matt sprinted for his car.

I followed as fast as I could go on my stilettos and pulled my gun from my purse, fully intending to protect Matt from any harm that might come to him.

He stopped beside his car. All four tires had been slashed. He glanced at me. "Why are you carrying a gun on our date?"

"I won't let someone shoot you like they did Ryan."

As if my words had woken him from some dream state, he took my pretty pink Glock from my hand and shoved me behind him. "Get down."

I crouched beside the car, pulling Matt down with me. "Do you see anyone?" I asked.

"No." He grinned. "If someone would have told me that I'd be hunkered down with a beautiful woman next to a disabled car, I would have said they were crazy. Life won't ever be boring with you around."

He stood and pulled me after him as we sprinted for the restaurant.

20

We barged through the restaurant doors and Matt motioned me to a seat in the waiting area. So much for a romantic evening.

I smiled at the sight of Matt, cell phone to his ear, and pink gun in his hand. He could make anything look manly.

"Maryann is coming to give us a ride home, the department is sending someone to take our statement, and I've called a tow truck." He sat beside me. "Are you okay? You looked a bit … shell shocked."

Ooops. Got caught staring with a goofy look on my face. "I'm fine. At least there weren't any bullets flying."

"I think they're sending a message for me to back off." He stretched his legs in front of him and crossed them at the ankles. "I must be getting close to solving this."

"We're getting close." I stared out the window in front of us.

A man, all in black, watched from the other side of the street. I grabbed my gun out of Matt's hand, and in my usual 'not thinking before acting', raced out the door toward him. "Stop! I will shoot you." Not really, but hopefully he didn't know that.

Matt thundered after, yelling my name. I ignored him and kept going. The man I chased dashed down the sidewalk, arms pumping. I kicked off my heels and kept running.

Maybe I really did need to go to the gym.

My breath came in painful gasps and a painful stitch in my side had me almost bent in two. Matt caught up with me in seconds and passed, giving chase. I loved that man. He didn't stop to question why I was chasing someone, only that I was, and must therefore have a reason. Sometimes that reason might be a bit off-the-wall, but I tended to trust my instincts.

"Wait." I stopped and leaned against a wall. Matt had left me behind. I took several deep breaths, and ran again.

My barefoot caught a ridge in the sidewalk. My ring toe snapped. I cried out and fell, sliding several feet on my stomach. My gun clattered into the street. Angela's dress ripped down the side. She was going to kill me, either that or I owed her a new wardrobe.

I sat up and glanced at my toe. It was already swollen, purple, and throbbing like a drum. My giving chase was over. My hands, raw from the sidewalk, and still showing some of the rash from the poison ivy burned as if I'd touched a hot stove.

Glancing around the dark sidewalk, and realizing I was very much alone, I got to my feet. If someone wanted to grab me, now was their chance. I hobbled to retrieve my gun, then headed back toward the restaurant as fast as my broken toe would allow.

Where was Matt? He was unarmed since I had so thoughtlessly taken my gun back. I hadn't heard sounds of a scuffle, and prayed he had either caught the man without a fight or the man had gotten clean away without harming my boyfriend.

I shuffled into the parking lot like a zombie, my scraped hands held out at my sides. My heels, which I'd retrieved on the way back, dangled from my fingers. Maryann and an officer I didn't know, rushed toward me.

"What happened?" Maryann grabbed my wrists. "Where's

my brother?”

“I fell, and he is chasing a suspect.”

“Which way?” The officer asked.

I pointed, and he raced away.

“Let’s get these scrapes cleaned up.” Maryann shouted for someone to bring water and clean cloths and sat me in the back seat of her car, my legs on the outside. “I miss all of the excitement.”

“We weren’t looking for it,” I said. “We were on a date.”

“I only have a few more months of teaching before I become your full time literary assistant. I intend to accompany you on all your sleuthing expeditions, which, in your case, is really research.”

“I hope there aren’t anymore,” I hissed as I lifted my dress, or what was left of it, above my knees.

“Don’t say that.” Her face fell. “I’ve always wanted to be like Nancy Drew.”

“I’m Nancy Drew. You’re her friend.”

She shrugged. “Whatever. The point is, my life is boring. Your’s isn’t.”

“You sound like Angela.” Did everyone seriously think being in danger for your life was fun?

“God forbid I’m anything like your sister.” She turned and took a bowl of ice water and cloth napkins from a waitress.

“Who in the heck were we chasing?” Matt leaned against the car, hardly sounding as if he’d just sped after someone.

I definitely needed to get in shape. “That guy was staring at us through the window. I think he might have been the one who slashed the tires.”

“Right.” He shook his head before taking over the washing of my scrapes from his sister. “That was foolish on both our parts.”

“Probably.” I brushed his hair off his forehead. “Thanks for not getting killed.”

He laughed. "When you took off out of the restaurant, I didn't think twice about following. You've guts of steel, Stormi."

"And a head as thick as a cement block."

He stood. "That, too. Stay here. I need to talk to the officers investigating my car. I'll come get you when I'm ready to leave."

Maryann returned the bowl and napkins, then climbed into the back seat with me. "Do you want me to call your family?"

"No, Mom will worry and Angela will start screaming about her dress."

"You really need to buy your own clothes."

I rested my head against the seat back, suddenly exhausted. "I know." My hands and knees stung, and I shivered in the dress that no longer kept away the winter chill. I lifted my bottom and wrapped in the blanket I had been sitting on.

My intentions for having a literary assistant did include research, mailings, setting up book signings, etc., not actually hitting the streets armed with a gun to solve crime. Matt wouldn't stand for it, and I hated to think of my best friend, I'd had so few close friends in life, in danger. Still, Maryann was an adult. If she wanted to follow me while I pounded the pavements, she would.

Matt returned a few minutes later. "The guy I chased was not much more than a kid. It wasn't Stinger, but he could have been the one who flattened my tires. I've given his description to the officers, and now I'm ready to go home." He got into the driver's seat. "I can pick my car up at the mechanics tomorrow."

"Home sounds really good right now." I closed my eyes.

Maryann climbed into the front with her brother. "When we moved to Oak Meadows, I thought we'd be bored silly."

She clicked her seatbelt. "Who knew small towns were so exciting."

"Stop it right there." Matt glared at her. "This is dangerous, not exciting."

"Stop being such a bully. Can't you see Stormi is in pain?"

Way to go, Maryann. I often wished I could distract Matt from the subject at hand as easily as she did.

We pulled into my driveway a few minutes later. I took a deep breath and opened the car door. I might as well face my sister's wrath and get it over with.

Matt helped me up the drive, my knees swelling and growing stiff, and into the house. Maryann carried my shoes, purse, and gun.

"For crying out loud." Angela stopped between the kitchen and the living room, a bowl of popcorn in her hands. "You are not allowed to borrow my clothes again."

"I'm fine, thanks for asking." I winced and made my way to the sofa.

"What happened?" Angela set the bowl in my lap. "You look like hell."

"I feel like it." I smiled. She might be the meanest sister on the planet, but she also knew popcorn was one of my comfort foods. "We were chasing a suspect that we think slashed Matt's tires. I broke my toe."

She gasped and dashed to the kitchen, yelling for Mom. "Stormi is hurt again!"

Angela returned with ice, Mom following, belting her robe around her waist. Mom put some of the ice in a baggy and plopped it on my toe.

"Ow!" I set a napkin between the ice and my foot.

"You, my daughter, are a walking disaster zone." Mom crossed her arms. "You're off your feet for a few days."

"Which is a good thing," Matt sat, sitting beside me. "She

won't be able to get into trouble if she can't get around."

"Could someone please tape my broken toe to the middle toe?" Where was the sympathy when someone was injured?

I also didn't have time for this. I could spend my mornings writing, but by the afternoon of each day, I'd be going stir crazy and wanting to get this case off my back. Maybe I could use crutches. No, I'd never been able to master the torture sticks. I'd have to wear sandals and walk on my heel. Where there was a will, there was a way.

"Look at her." Mom shook her head. "She's trying to work out in her mind how she can snoop with that foot. She's hopeless."

Matt grabbed a handful of popcorn. I hated sharing my popcorn. "God definitely broke the mold when he made her."

"I'm right here." I shifted so the bowl was on the other side of me, out of his reach.

"I can see that, dear." Mom pulled some medical tape out of the pocket of her robe and knelt in front of me. "It seems like I've been doing a lot of taping you up over the years."

"Just call me Graceful."

She scoffed. "Foolish is more like it." She cut the tape to size, then gentle positioned the injured appendage against the toe next to it. "Were the bumps and bruises worth it?"

"Matt?"

"All we have is another suspect." He tried reaching for another handful of popcorn. I pushed it farther away. "Hey," he said. "I thought you loved me."

"I do, but I don't share my popcorn."

"Nope. She never has." Angela brought in another bowl and handed it to Matt. "But, I do."

"I'm sorry about the evening," I said, meeting Matt's gaze.

"I'm not. If I have to run down dark streets, there is no one I'd rather do it with than you."

"How sweet." Maryann shoved her hand in his bowl. "We need a plan. Now that Stormi is injured, we need to divvy up the responsibilities."

Matt groaned. "The police will handle things from here." He muttered something about saying the right things, but wasting his breath.

"He's right," I said. "We can't all go off running up and down the streets to catch a killer."

"Thank you." He looked at me as if I'd grown horns and felt my forehead.

I slapped his hand away. "Stop it. I'm just saying that too many people out asking questions isn't very subtle."

Whatever I couldn't do, Greta could. We'd come up with a plan in the morning. We could rent another wheelchair if we had to. One way or the other, I was putting an end to the crime before it put an end to me.

21

I called Greta the next morning, after waking to find that Mom had already left for the day. She agreed to pick me up around lunch time and take me to Mom's shop so we could discuss our next step.

Managing to get a sock on my foot, I struggled into some sweats, trying not to lean too much to one side and step down, then took the steps one at a time until I was on the ground floor. All I'd managed to do, other than get dressed, was to tie my hair back into a ponytail. My entire body ached from its contact with the sidewalk.

After making myself a mug of coffee, and saying goodbye to the kids who had to return to school, I grabbed a package of powdered doughnuts and made the painful return trip up the stairs to do some writing. My inbox showed several emails from my agent, checking on the progress of the book. If she only knew. I responded that I was making progress, then pulled up an empty word document which I titled suspects.

I put Reed at the top and Stinger in parenthesis. Then, I listed Ivy, Ginger, and Sissy. I left Lacey off. My gut told me she was guilty of nothing more than creating her hybrids. The girl seemed as elusive as her attempt to come up with a "never before created flower."

We really needed to follow Ivy for a few days to find out who her gentleman friend was. Find him, we would find

Stinger, I was certain.

The sound of a lawn mower pulled me to the window. I'd almost forgotten that Rusty had returned as my gardener. I'd need to write him a check. Next door, Tony Salazar waved, trying to get Rusty's attention. Every time Rusty circled in that direction, he'd turn his head. What was up with the guy now?

Sadie chased after the lawn mover, barking her fool head off. Mom must have let her out before leaving for work. I sighed. I'd have to hobble down the stairs again.

"Hey, Tony!" I waved as I stepped out the back door.

"Can you get him to turn that off and talk to me?"

I limped to Rusty's side and tapped his shoulder. He turned with wide-eyes.

"Why won't you talk to Tony?"

Rusty shrugged. "He wants me to cut his lawn. He doesn't want to pay enough."

Ah. "Wait here." I made my way to the fence. "Are you offering him something other than ten dollars to mow your yard?"

"Yeah. I offered him a hundred-and-twenty-five dollars a month to keep my yard up. He insists on ten dollars. Now, he won't speak to me because he says I'm robbing him."

"He doesn't understand. I agreed to ten, but pay him more. Just tell him what he wants to hear."

"Okay." He started to hop off his ladder, then turned back to me. "You haven't been doing much of the neighborhood watch."

I shook my head. "I'm sorry about that. Some other things have claimed my attention."

"I've heard. I thought you might want to know that other than your watchdogs, there is a red Cadillac that cruises past your place several times a night."

"Oh." I glanced toward the street. Since I didn't know

anyone with a red Cadillac, and most security people drove automobiles that didn't stand out, it had to be one of Stinger's people. It looked as if I'd be staring out of my window that night. "Thanks. I'll clarify things with Rusty for you."

I returned to Rusty. "He'll pay you ten dollars."

He nodded. "I don't like being robbed."

"I understand. Who takes care of your finances?"

He looked confused.

"Your money. Who pays your bills?"

"Mama used to. Now she has an old man who makes me give him my money, then he gives me fifty back to buy candy with. I told him I wanted ten!" He tensed.

"I'm sure you did. He's giving you plenty to buy candy with. Who buys your food or clothes?"

"The church. I love overalls."

I was relieved to know that someone was looking out for my friend. I made a mental note to find out who his accountant was. "Have you seen anything lately?"

He nodded.

As usual, I'd have to drag it from him. "Can you tell me what? Have you seen any strangers?"

"The streets are busy at night."

"What do you mean?" I plopped onto a lawn chair to take weight off my legs.

"Cars, people, all going up and down the street, like zombies."

"Zombies?"

"They don't talk."

I sighed. I wasn't going to get any information out of him today. "I need to get back to work. We'll talk later."

"The zombies carry guns, Miss Stormi."

I froze halfway out of my chair. "You stay away from them." I would definitely be spending time at my window tonight. Mrs. Olsen had nothing on me when it came to nosiness. I glanced across the street to where she pretended to water flowers that weren't there. I changed direction and slowly crossed the street.

"Hello."

"What do you want?" She turned, narrowly missing me with the hose spray.

"I know you're one of the most concerned residents on this street, and since I'm the head of the Neighborhood Watch, I'm wondering whether you've seen anything that might concern you."

"Cut the hogwash." She turned off the water. "Everyone knows you've gotten yourself into another fix. Because of you, this street isn't safe to walk down once the lights go off."

"Do you feel in danger?"

"I keep my doors locked and my curtains closed."

"Have you called the police?"

"Why?" She grabbed a rake from near the porch. "They don't do anything except walk back and forth. There's no law against that, unless they're underage of course. Not that I'm going to be the one to go outside and ask them."

"Zombies," I whispered.

"What's that?" She frowned.

"Oh, nothing. Have a good day." I turned and limped back home.

If Stinger was trying to intimidate me, why isn't he making more sure that it's me seeing his people rather than my neighbors? Before now, I'd had no idea the danger was literally in my front yard. I stopped with one hand on the doorknob and turned to stare at the security detail across the street. Were they concerned at all that non-residents were wandering the neighborhood?

My poor legs were getting way more exercise than they

should. I crossed the street again. The SUV was empty. I scratched my head. Was the vehicle only for show? It wasn't working very well as a deterrent if Rusty and Mrs. Olsen were to be believed. Where were the security people?

I opened the door and almost fell back from the stench. It was obvious no one had opened the door in a few days. Blood spatter covered the two front seats and parts of the dash. I gagged and glanced at Matt's house. His car still sat in the driveway. Hopefully, that meant he was home.

Leaving the door open, I went to Matt's house and banged on the door. He opened it, looking finer than he had in his dress clothes the night before. He stood there, toothbrush in hand, and dressed in nothing more than a pair of flannel lounge pants.

"Oh." I put a hand over my heart to keep it from beating free. "Yeah, um, the security guys are missing and their vehicle is full of blood."

"Repeat that."

I tore my gaze away from his chest and repeated my words. "There's also talk of zombies, I mean, strangers, walking the street at night."

He thrust his toothbrush in my hand and pushed past me, running barefoot and bare chested to the SUV. He stopped and put his forearm over his nose and mouth. By the time I got there, he had gained a bit of composure. "Call the police, Mrs. Olsen."

"Put some clothes on Mr. Steele!"

"Please." He cut her a stern look. "I'm asking as an officer of the law."

She huffed and headed inside.

He ran his fingers through his hair. "I haven't checked on them in days. This is my fault."

"Wouldn't their supervisor have wondered something?"

"That is curious. Would you mind waiting here while I

grab my cell phone and some clothes?"

I shook my head and sat on the curb. Sirens wailed in the distance, the sound becoming too familiar.

Rusty pushed his lawn-mower across the street and stopped by the SUV. "Zombies," he said.

I was tempted to agree with him. I wrapped my arms around my knees and rested my chin on them. This was the weirdest case I'd ever gotten mixed up in. If Stinger knew where I lived, if he was worried about me getting close, why not just come and get me? None of it made any sense.

Two squad cars pulled up, one on each side of the SUV, blocking the street, and turned off their sirens. "Where's the officer on scene?"

"I'm here." Matt ran up, now wearing jeans and a flannel shirt. Poor guy, getting called to work on his day off. He explained that I was the one who had discovered the blood-filled automobile.

I sighed and headed for my house. I wasn't in the mood to give a statement. I wasn't in the mood for the neighbors to stare through their windows, and I definitely wasn't in the mood to be looked at by the police as if I were somehow responsible. They could come and get my statement, or better yet, send Matt. My legs hurt and Greta would be picking me up very soon. It was another day with no writing.

Once inside my house, I headed straight for the pantry and pulled out the makings of a cheese and broccoli casserole. Cooking soothed me, and it had been way too long since I'd filled my freezer. It wasn't until a tear dropped on my hand as I reached for a can of cream of chicken soup that I realized I was crying.

Matt's arms wrapped around my waist and he pulled me to my chest. "Shhh. What's wrong?"

"People keep dying." I hadn't heard him come in. "No one is safe around me."

"This isn't your fault. Those men were professionals."

"If so, and they couldn't stay alive, then why am I? It's almost as if Stinger's hands are tied against me and all he's able to do is intimidate."

"That is strange." His chest rumbled under my cheek. "Come sit down."

"I'm cooking."

"Come." He led me to the living room and sat me on the sofa. "You're exhausted, in pain, and distraught. Take a nap."

"But Greta is coming in an hour."

"Why?" His eyes narrowed.

"To take me to the shop."

"Are you telling the truth?

"Yes." She *was* taking me to the shop. It's where we planned to go after there that he didn't want to know about. "Can you call her and tell her to come in two hours instead?"

"Gladly. I'll get your statement later this evening." He pulled an Afghan over me. "I love you." He kissed me.

I was asleep before he was out the door.

The banging on the front door and Sadie's barking woke me. I silently thanked Matt for letting the dog in and crawled stiffly from the sofa. I started to open the door when my cell phone rang. I recognized the number as Starr's.

"Hello?"

"Where are you?"

"I'm at home. Why?"

"I just heard about a red head being fished out of the lake and thought it was you. No worries." Click.

I stared at the phone as I opened the door to let Greta in. "Starr, who didn't sound like Starr, but sort of did sound like her, thought I had been killed and tossed in the lake. Now, why would a prostitute I'd just met care whether I was alive or dead?"

22

"I think we're surrounded by people who aren't who they say they are," Greta said. She held up a fast food bag. "I brought lunch. Let's go spy on some people."

"Do you mind if we run by the hospital first? I'd like to visit Ryan." I grabbed my purse, slapped a baseball cap on my head, and set the alarm.

We ate on the way. Greta's driving was erratic enough that I had to reach several times for the "Oh, crap" handle that hung to my right. Eating and driving were not two things she did together well. By the time we arrived in the hospital parking lot, the food in my stomach was well-shaken and my shoulders tense.

"Let's make this quick. Ann is already mad that I left her to mind the store. She wanted to come with us."

"I'm sure she did, but there is no reason to close shop to do a stakeout." I exited the van on shaky legs and made my way, stiffly, to the double glass doors.

"Still sore after last night, huh?" Greta caught up with me with little effort. "You should have taken a hot bath. Works every time on these old bones of mine."

"I'll remember that if there's a next time."

She laughed. "Girl, we're talking about you. There will definitely be a next time."

"Shut up." I entered the hospital and made a beeline for

the elevator.

Greta's cackling followed me inside. I put my finger over the button to close the doors and raised my eyebrows. Her eyes widened.

"You wouldn't."

"I'm pretty sure I would." I grinned and pushed the button.

She slid through, the door bouncing open as it hit against her plump hips. "Not funny."

I shrugged.

The elevator dinged and the doors swung open when we reached Ryan's floor. A tall black woman wearing a floppy hat and stilettos, took one look at us and made a dash for the stairs.

"Ivy!" I started to run after her, then thought of Ryan. What if she had harmed him? I glanced toward his room, dismayed to see Reed wasn't at his post. Despite the warning looks cast my way from the nurse's station, I limp-ran to Ryan's room and came to a skid inside.

Ryan sat up, a tray of food in front of him. "What's wrong?"

"I should be asking you that." I sat painfully in the closest chair. "Where is Reed? Why was Ivy here?"

"Oh." He sighed and pushed his tray away as Greta entered. "I'm uh, well, I'm seeing her."

"What? I thought she was Stinger's woman." I gasped. "Oh, Ryan."

He shook his head. "I'm not Stinger."

"You're a cop dating a prostitute?" Greta crossed her arms. "Now, I've heard everything."

"I'm not the first." His face darkened.

"You know who Stinger is, don't you?" I pointed my finger at him. "I thought you were one of the good guys." The clamping of his lips told me everything I needed to know. My heart ached. "I'm glad you and Angela didn't start seeing each other." I pushed to my feet. "Let's go, Greta."

I needed to leave before he saw my tears.

"Wait."

I took a deep, shuddering breath without looking back.

"Why do you think you're still alive, Stormi? Think about it. I'm your friend. I would never harm you."

I squared my shoulders and left. A man whom I had thought to be a close friend had betrayed me. Not only me, but his partner. Matt would be devastated.

I knew better than to force Ryan to tell me Stinger's identity. I was pretty sure I knew who it was anyway. A friend of the gang's or not, if he told me, Ryan's life would be in grave danger. I couldn't have that on my conscience, betrayal or not.

The tears fell, blurring my vision. I held the elevator for Greta, and wiped my face on my sleeve.

"That was informative," she said, pressing the button for the lobby. "What are we going to do with the information?"

"I'll have to tell Matt. But, first, we have a stakeout to do."

"On who? There's no sense watching Ivy anymore."

"There is still the matter of the poison ivy."

"Right."

When the elevator doors open, we almost ran into Reed, his hands full with two cups of coffee. "What's wrong?" He asked, looking at me.

"Nothing. I'm not feeling well." I wiped my face again. "We're just leaving." I pushed past him, glancing back when we reached the doors to the outside.

Reed watched us leave, his dark face impassive. "Be careful," he called.

I wasn't sure whether he was warning us or actually showing concern for our welfare. I chose to go with the warning. We were close to catching Stinger and shutting down the gang. Things were going to get ugly.

"I'm wondering who the dead woman with red hair is," I said, clicking my seatbelt. "Do you think it could be Ginger?"

"That's a good guess." Greta started the van and pulled from the lot. "See if Matt will tell you."

I fished my cell phone from my purse and dialed. "Who is the woman found in the lake last night?"

"Hello to you, too." He sighed. "How did you find out about that?"

"A celestial being told me."

He groaned. "It's Ginger."

I nodded at Greta. "Okay, thanks, and Matt?"

"Yeah?"

"I need to tell you something, but not over the phone. Can you come by tonight? I'll call you when I get home."

"Sure. Where are you going now?"

"Love you, bye." I hung up, not wanting to tell him I was going on a stakeout. He'd only fuss, even though it was the middle of the day. What could possibly go wrong other than people lying for months to someone who thought them a friend?

Enough crying. It wouldn't change anything. There was work to be done. "Head to Melrose Street," I said. "If nothing is happening there, we'll go to Ivy's mother's house."

"That's as good of a plan as any."

Fifteen minutes later, we parked in front of a closed video rental store.

I didn't bother stuffing my hair under my cap. The gang knew who I was and that I was asking questions.

The usual girls stood on the street corner. I never understood that. I always thought their profession took place in the dark of night. I spotted Ivy and Sissy in what looked like a heated argument. With arms waving, they shouted at each. We were too far away to hear what they were saying.

"Those are our main suspects," Greta said. "I'd give anything to be an ant on the sidewalk right about now."

Ivy stormed away and climbed into a rusted Volkswagon. "Follow her," I said. "Try not to be seen."

"She's too mad to see much of anything." Greta whipped the van after her.

Ivy went straight to her mother's house, exited the car, and marched to the greenhouse. I opened my door and followed.

She turned as she opened the greenhouse door. "You're a piece of work." She stepped inside.

Since she hadn't ordered me to leave, I stepped into the humidity. "Did you kill Daisy?"

"Don't be ridiculous. I'm dating a cop, which I'm sure you know now."

"So? Why is Ryan's word so important that I'm still alive?"

She plucked a wilted leaf off of a rose bush. "If I tell you that, I'll be as dead as Ginger."

"Why is she dead?" I leaned against the counter after making sure no poison ivy was anywhere in sight.

"Because she knew too much and was blackmailing Stinger." She glared. "Stop being so stupid already. You must know everything you need to know." She jabbed her finger in my forehead. "Think with that addled brain God gave you."

I had all the information? Then, why wasn't it falling into place? If Ivy didn't kill Daisy, and I actually believed her when she said she didn't, then … Oh!" I whirled and rushed back to the van. "Back to Melrose. Hurry."

"What did she say?"

"That I had all the information I needed to crack this thing wide open. She's right."

"Tell me."

"Not until I know for certain."

"That's just plain mean." She sped back to Melrose. Sissy was nowhere to be seen.

My shoulders slumped. "Do we know where Sissy lives?"

"I can find out." She turned the wheel and took us to Heavenly Bakes.

Mom glanced up from where she frosted a cake. She wiped her hands on her apron. "Spill the beans. What did you find out?"

I told her about Ryan and Ivy, about my suspicions regarding Sissy and Reed, and about Rusty's zombies. When I'd finished, she stared at me, her lips pressed tight together as she processed the information.

"That's quite the day you two have had," she said, picking up her spatula. "Considering all that, and the danger involved, I'm kind of glad I stayed here, and I'm doubly glad your sister didn't get her wish about going out with that no-good, dirty cop."

Considering how much time Ryan had spent at our house over the last few months, I knew she was feeling as injured and betrayed as I was. My mom always prided herself on her ability to read people at a glance. We'd both failed this time.

I was a writer. I was supposed to notice these things, to see inside a person as fodder for my stories. Pain ripped through me like a knife. "I need to head home and prepare myself for telling Matt."

"I'll drop you off," Greta said. "Then come back here and see what I can find out on Sissy."

"I need coffee first." I headed across the street.

"Gracious, girl." Sarah stopped me as soon as I entered the coffee shop. "If you want people to buy your books, you should at least look presentable when going out in public. Sweat pants?"

"I'm not in the mood, Sarah." I got in line.

"No need to be snippy. I'm only trying to help."

"Do you have something to tell me? If not, go back to your table." I'd regret my rude behavior later.

"That gardener of yours is in jail."

"What?" I frowned. "How is that even possible?"

She shrugged. "He hit someone over the head with a shovel."

I paid for my coffee, waited for the Barista to fill my order, then hurried back to Greta. Since she had driven that day, I didn't have a vehicle. I quickly explained what Sarah had told me. Greta agreed to drive me to the station.

Once there, I approached the desk where Angela sat talking on the phone. I tapped her head. She held up a finger, telling me to wait.

"I will not wait." I hung up the phone.

"Hey!"

"That was a personal call." From the look on her face, I had guessed right. "Where's Rusty?"

"Locked up."

"Has bail been posted?"

She shrugged. "He assaulted someone, Stormi."

"In self-defense, I'm sure."

She sighed. "Talk to your boyfriend. I just work here."

"Please, I've had a rough day. I'm sorry I hung up the phone."

She cocked her head. "You do look a little … rough. Matt is in his office. Go on back."

"Thank you." I turned to Greta. "I'll catch a ride home with Matt or Angela." Ignoring the stiffening in my knees from too much activity, I headed for Matt's office where he scowled at something someone said on the phone.

"I don't care what your intentions are, Linda. I expect you to remain professional and do your job!" He slammed the receiver down, noticing me in the doorway. He jumped to his feet and rushed to my side. "What happened?"

"You might want to sit down for this."

23

"You look like you need to sit down." He led me to a chair in front of his desk, then pulled another seat close. "What is it you want to tell me? Is this what you were going to say tonight?"

I nodded. "I don't know a good way to tell you this, so I'll just say it." I told him of my visits to Ryan and to Ivy.

He listened with a stony face, then stood and paced the room. "I was beginning to suspect Ryan knew more than he was telling, but this is more than I thought."

"What are you going to do?"

"I don't know. If I tell the chief, he could go to jail or worse, dead. At the minimum, he'll have to turn in his badge." He rubbed his hands down his face. "This is so hard to believe. We've been partners for a long time."

"I'm so sorry." I stared at my hands in my lap, giving him a moment to come to terms with what I'd said. When he returned to his seat, I asked, "What happened with Rusty?"

"He found someone snooping around your house and hit them with a shovel. The boy will be all right, and isn't going to press charges, the little idiot, even though he is spending the night in the hospital. He knows he was in the wrong by trespassing. The chief just wants Rusty to have some time to learn that peeping, and assaulting, is wrong."

"He was only looking out for me."

Matt nodded. "I know."

"Has he told you about the zombies?"

His head jerked up. "He said something about the boy he hit was one, but I chalked it up to Rusty's crazy talk."

"Mrs. Olsen also said the street is very active at night. I plan on staying up to see what is going on. I think the zombies are people keeping an eye on me."

"It looks as if I'll be sitting up with you. I'll bring pizza."

"Maybe we should observe from your house. If we do it at mine, we'll have a crowd." I stood and caressed his face. "I'll see you in a few hours."

He nodded, leaning into my touch. "I'll call when I get home."

I brushed a kiss across his lips and went to ask Angela to give me a ride home.

"Seriously? After the way you hung up on my phone call? Fine." She glanced at the clock. "I don't get off work for another thirty minutes. Have a seat." She waved me toward some hard plastic chairs bolted to the floor.

"Get your hands off me!" A police officer, one hand clamped firmly on Starr's upper arm, dragged her down the hallway. "You've got the wrong girl."

She glanced at me and winked. Who was this person?

The officer dragged her down the hall and practically threw her into a conference room. I met Angela's bored gaze.

"Welcome to the precinct." She returned to her work.

Starr pounded on the window a few times, then moved out of sight. Everything in me wanted to go into that room and ask her who she was, but the presence of the officer outside the room deterred me. I'd seen enough trouble for one day.

Matt came out of his office and entered the conference room. Now, I really wanted to go in.

"Let's go." Angela grabbed her purse.

Time sure passed quickly at the police station. I couldn't

believe half an hour had come and gone. I followed my sister to her second-hand BMW and slid behind the driver's wheel.

"Please don't come into my place of work dressed the way you are," she said. "I have a certain standard to uphold."

"Why is everyone concerned with my dressing habits?"

"You look like a homeless person."

"My knees are skinned up. Loose fitting sweat pants are comfortable."

We pulled into the driveway. She turned toward me. "You look terrible, Stormi. You need to get some rest. Take a long soak in the tub. Anything that will make you look more … alive. You're ragged. Mom is worried about you."

"Just Mom?"

"Fine." She exhaled sharply. "We all are. Why can't you just stick to your writing?"

"I honestly don't know why life won't let me. Maybe I have a gift." I exited the car.

"A gift for finding trouble," she said, after joining me outside.

We walked in silence to the house. I disarmed the alarm and headed upstairs. That bath sounded wonderful. I filled the tub with hot water and bubbles smelling like roses. I would have preferred something that didn't remind me of Ivy's greenhouse.

I shed my clothes and climbed in, taking a sharp breath at the heat of the water. I slowly lowered myself into the bubbles, feeling the heat start to ease the tenseness in my body. I leaned back and closed my eyes.

A ringing coming from my purse woke me. The water was cold, and I shivered as I reached for my purse.

"Hello?"

"It's me. Are you ready?"

"Oh, sure. Give me five minutes." I hung up on Matt and climbed from the tub, rubbing the goose pimples on my skin away with a towel. I chose another pair of sweats to cover my scrapes, brushed out my hair and went downstairs. "Going to Matt's!" I called, in case anyone was home to hear me.

With Mom now living in the basement, and Angela overseeing improvements to the attic, my home had returned mostly to the quiet tomb it once was. Of course, renovations in the attic were on hold at the moment. With all that was going on, I didn't want strangers traipsing in and out of my house.

In case any zombies were watching, I clipped a leash on Sadie's collar and snuck us out the back door. Not that my giant, scared-of-her- own-shadow, dog would be much help against an attacker, but her presence still soothed me as I kept to the shadows on my way to Matt's place. That and the gun in my purse.

A few people, dressed in dark clothes, ambled up and down the street. I watched for a minute, thoroughly confused. They made no attempt to hide themselves, just walked up and back, up and back. I wanted to wave my hand in front of a young man's face as he passed the bush I crouched behind, but kept my hands firmly on Sadie's leash. She growled. The guy passed as if he hadn't heard her. What the heck?

I stepped out of hiding. As one, all six of them turned to stare. I expected to be riddled with bullets. Instead, they turned and resumed their pacing. Weird and freaky.

Matt stepped off his front porch. "Isn't that the strangest thing?"

"Not so strange." Ryan stepped from around the house.

"What are you doing out of the hospital?" I started to rush to him, but remembered what a traitor he was.

"Let's just say I let myself out." He held one arm close to his side. "These are my people. They're here for your protection."

"You're asking for a gang war on a family street." Matt balled his hands at his side, clearly restraining himself from punching his former partner.

"Stinger doesn't want a war any more than we do." Ryan sat on the porch steps. "I'm sorry, man. I couldn't tell you what I was messed up in. It wasn't even something to be concerned about until the gangs moved in. I thought I could get them to leave and no one the wiser."

"Who is Stinger?" Matt stepped toward him.

"If I tell you that, I can't protect you."

"If you don't tell us, we can't stop him. Eventually, he'll move on and do the same thing somewhere else. People are dying!"

"Prostitutes and gang members."

"They're still people," I said. "Ryan, please. Is Reed Stinger?"

He nodded. "He's my cousin. My family doesn't turn against blood. Other than keeping Stormi and her family safe, despite her nosing around, my hands are tied in all this."

"You have to turn yourself in to the chief." Matt leaned against the porch. "You'll lose your badge."

"It's fine." Ryan took a deep breath. "I'll become a private investigator or something." He pushed to his feet. "Keep Rusty in jail until this is all over. I'll get rid of Stinger."

"How?" I crossed my arms.

"I'll deal with it. That's all you need to know." He strolled back around the side of the house and out of view.

"Can we trust him?" I asked.

"You're still alive, aren't you?"

Why did people keep saying that? Couldn't the fact that I wasn't dead have a little something to do with my abilities?

"You don't think he'll do something stupid, do you?"

Matt held out his hand. "I have no idea. Let's eat." He led me into the house.

Maryann stepped back from the window. "Was that Ryan? Why isn't he coming in?"

I glanced at Matt for approval before telling her about their friend. He nodded that it was okay, I explained the latest findings while we set paper plates on the table.

"Oh." She slumped into a chair. "Hmm. I never would have guessed that."

"Yeah, it's a shocker." I was still reeling, and I'd had several hours to get used to the idea.

"I don't think my brother will recover from this," she said, setting out glasses of iced tea.

"I'm fine." Matt sat at the head of the table. "He's not all bad. He's been looking out for my girl." He gave me a sad smile. "He'll make a great PI."

I grabbed a slice of pepperoni and sausage pizza. "Why was Starr dragged into the station today?"

"Because she can't keep her mouth shut." Matt frowned. "I'll tell you all about her in a few days. Right now, I'm starving."

I met Maryann's gaze and shrugged. While most of the time I'd been known to press for an answer, I figured my sweetheart had endured enough for one day. After supper, I planned on kissing him until he forgot all the bad things that had happened that day.

After we finished eating and stored the leftovers in the refrigerator, Matt led me to his front porch. "Two nights in a row we're able to grab a few minutes alone. Whatever will we do?"

"I have a few things in mind." I led him to a porch swing that matched the one on my porch and wrapped in a quilt he kept there, pulling one corner aside in invitation. "Wanna neck?"

His teeth flashed in the moonlight. "Now what kind of a fool do you think I am? Of course, I do." He slid under the blanket with me and tilted my face to meet his.

We weren't exactly alone, not with Ryan's goons patrolling the street, but the evergreen bushes that shaded Matt's porch in the summertime, helped hide us in the winter. Soon, Matt was kissing my neck, nibbling my earlobes, and making me forget the pain of the past day. Here, I had thought I would be helping him.

It didn't take long before the quilt lay in a puddle at our feet. Having reverted back to our teenage years with the heavy petting, we'd warmed ourselves right up. My breath short, I came up for air. "Wow."

Matt rested his head against mine. "Yeah. We'd better go inside. I'm sure the neighbors are having a field day watching the show."

I giggled. "The only one who will care is Mrs. Olsen." I stood and folded the quilt.

The intensity of desire for him scared me. Since I'd held to the vow I made years ago, maybe alone time with Matt wasn't a good idea. We were getting dangerously close to a line I wasn't ready to cross.

"Matt!" Maryann stood in the doorway. "Ryan's been shot. He didn't make it." She burst into sobs.

I slipped my hand in Matt's and held on tight. We'd just lost our protection and a good friend.

24

After staying up late mourning the loss of Ryan, who it appears had tried to take on his cousin alone, I headed to the coffee shop for the largest blended frozen coffee they had. My eyes were gritty and swollen from crying and lack of sleep. I still couldn't believe he was gone.

Detective Ryan Koontz might not have been exactly who we thought he was, but he had tried his best to do right by Matt and me. For that, I loved him.

I choked back tears and parked in front of the coffee shop, not caring that I took up two spaces. I glanced at Greta, who, now that Ryan was gone, vowed to never leave my side until the gang leader was behind bars. While I appreciated the gesture, I wanted to be alone with my thoughts.

"Do you want anything?" I asked.

"No. Just make it quick. Windows don't stop bullets."

I nodded and headed into the shop. As usual the line was long. What wasn't usual, was the absence of Sarah typing one of her smut books at the table in the corner. The mood was subdued, whispered words of Ryan's passing. Elaborated stories on his death, touching on everything from a violent shootout to taking his own life. Mom had closed her store for the duration.

In reality, he'd been shot, execution style. I wanted to yell for everyone to shut up, go home, and lock their doors.

Exactly what I had planned until everything was over.

The minute Ryan's death had become known, the "zombies" had scattered like dust in the wind. I pressed my arm close to my chest where I'd chosen to stash my gun. Keeping it in my purse was no longer an option and the bulky sweatshirt I wore effectively hid the weapon. It probably wasn't the smartest move coming out for coffee, but locking myself in a prison would only drive me crazy. I'd promised to only go into crowded places when I felt the need for a bit of freedom. Matt had reluctantly agreed, as long as I didn't go alone and went straight to my destination and back.

Loaded down with coffee for me and my mother, I rejoined Greta in the jeep, and put the drinks in the cup holders. "Ready for confinement?"

"That sounds pretty good to me at this point. While Delicious Aroma might be packed, the streets look like a ghost town. It gives me the creeps."

I nodded and steered toward home. On the outskirts of my neighborhood, Sissy darted into the street and flagged us down. "Do I stop?"

"What if she's in trouble?" Greta rolled down her window. "You being chased?"

"Yes." She ran up to the car. "Please let me in."

She yanked open the passenger door, whipped a nine-millimeter from her pocket and whacked Greta in the head. Grabbing Greta's arm, she pulled her from the jeep, letting her fall to the road, before turning the gun on me. "Drive."

"Did you kill her?"

Sissy shrugged. "Don't know, don't care. Drive or I will shoot you right here where that handsome cop can come across your body."

I sighed. "Where to?"

"The warehouse district."

I whipped the jeep around and spun gravel taking us in the

directions she'd ordered. "I knew it was you. You got the poison ivy from Ivy's greenhouse."

"Well, aren't you just the smartest white woman I've ever met."

"Why Daisy?"

She cut me a sideways glance. "It isn't a secret on the streets that I'm Stinger's woman. She caught us together, recognized him, and threatened to go to the cops."

"Ginger?"

"Another smart white woman."

"You can drop the racial slurs, now." I slowed the jeep's speed, hoping, praying, Greta would be able to go for help. "They don't help."

"Reed is Stinger, right?"

"Yep, not that it's going to matter to you. Turn right up here." She directed me to pull in front of an abandoned building with boarded up windows.

"We thought this stupid little town would be the perfect center of operation. Now, once we dispose of the threats, we've got to move on. No more law enforcement for my man. Get out and don't try anything. I'm a good shot."

I climbed from the jeep and stood while Sissy climbed over the gearshift after me.

"Can I at least get my purse and my coffee?"

"I'll get them." She slung my purse over her shoulder and handed me one of the coffees.

I thought for a moment about throwing it in her face, but a frozen drink wouldn't do anything more than make her angry. I sipped at the melting slush. Maybe the caffeine would give me courage. At that moment, I was in short supply.

She peered in my purse. "Where's that stupid pink gun of yours?"

"I didn't think I would need it just getting coffee."

She cocked her head. "Maybe you aren't as bright as I gave you credit for. Let's go." She waved her gun toward a battered gray door in the side of the building.

My knees shook. I couldn't go in there. If I went in, I'd never come back out. I watched gangster movies. I knew what happened in warehouses. "Are you going to torture me? I don't have any information to give you."

"What are you talking about?"

"Nothing." I held my cup so tight some of the coffee spilled through the straw hole.

Sissy guided me to a large room that smelled strongly of cigarette smoke. Two metal chairs sat in the middle of the otherwise empty room. A woman with blond hair, head hanging, occupied one of them. My steps faltered.

"Sit there beside the stupid cop." Sissy shoved me into the chair. "I hope you're done with that coffee. I'm taking it so I can tie you up."

"Why? I can't go anywhere. You have a gun. Let me finish, at least." I needed to stall until I could get my hand in my bra and pull out my gun.

Sissy cut some twine from a roll on the floor and bound my feet to the legs of the chair. "I guess you can't run with a chair tied to you."

Twine? Seriously? I could rip through that in an hour. I thought the favored method of tying someone up was those plastic zip ties.

"Wake up, cop." Sissy kicked the woman next to me. "You've got company." She moved to a corner of the room and pulled a cell phone from her pocket.

While she called someone, Reed most likely, I peered at the woman next to me. She lifted her head and forced a smile through split lips. "Starr?" My blood ran cold. "You're a cop? You don't look old enough to be out of high school."

One eye was swollen shut, and her left cheek sported a

dark bruise. Oh, God, they *were* going to torture me.

"Looking young is what helped me infiltrate the ring. My name is Linda. Glad to meet you."

The same Linda that Matt was yelling at on the phone?

"We have to get out of here," I whispered. "They're going to kill us."

"I know that, but they took my gun."

"I have one in my bra."

"What?" She laughed, splitting her lip again.

I couldn't tear my gaze away from the spot of blood dripping onto her tee shirt. "She searched my purse, but didn't frisk me."

"Yeah, that one is dumber than a pile of fingernail clippings."

"Who beat you?"

"Not her. Reed did it. We have to get loose before he returns. I almost have my hands free. Once I do that, I'll retrieve your weapon and get us out of here."

Retrieve it? Oh, Lord, have mercy. I pulled against my restraints.

"You two have fun." Sissy wiggled her fingers at us. "Stinger will be here in an hour, then we'll have some fun."

"She's crazy, that one. I'm going to bounce my chair around and you untie—"

"Oops." Sissy came back into the room. "Almost forgot."

She took my cup and tossed it in the corner, then tied my hands behind my back. "Leaving you untied would not have been a good thing. My man would have been so mad." She patted my cheek, rather roughly, and then practically skipped from the room.

We only had an hour to get away. No one knew where we were. If Greta wasn't dead, she had probably been found by now and alerted Matt, but how would they know where to find us? My cell phone. Months ago, Matt had installed a

GPS on my phone because of my constantly getting into fixes such as the one I was in now.

"She left my phone." I grinned. "Matt will find us."

"Will he find us in time?" She yanked against the twine on her wrists hard enough to break a sweat.

"Your wrists are bleeding. If you keep pulling like that, you'll break them." I maneuvered my way around and worked at the twine. Her blood soon coated my fingers, making them slippery. *Concentrate, Stormi. You can do this.* They were almost shredded. Another good yank or two, and she would be free.

Footsteps echoed outside the door. I hurried to put my chair back where it belonged and hung my head. If someone were to come in at that time, with Linda and I as close as we were to getting free, I didn't think I could look sufficiently cowed.

The footsteps receded. I took a deep breath and let it out long and slow, trying to keep the panic at bay. "Koontz is dead," I said.

She huffed. "I know. I was there. He recognized me, right before he was shot. His silent mouthing of my real name tipped off Reed. I don't wish him dead, but he was mixed up in something dirty he should never have gotten involved in."

"Reed is his cousin."

She glanced at me through her one working eye. "I wouldn't have covered for my cousin if they were anything like Reed."

"Me either. Still, he was my friend and my protector. I won't be happy that he's gone."

Drinking the coffee was a very bad idea. My bladder screamed for release. I squirmed on my chair and felt the bindings around my feet loosen. Hope blossomed. I spread my legs as far as they would go, again and again, the fibers of the twine biting into my ankles. If I could get my feet free…

I paused when more footsteps sounded outside the door. "When they come in," I said. "Yank hard for all your worth. Our lives depend on it." I got my feet free and stood. Painfully, my still healing scrapes screaming, I slipped my legs through my arms and worked on the ties around my wrists with my teeth. More footsteps.

Either Sissy was pacing or the entire gang was arriving. I chewed faster, sharp pieces of thread poking my tongue.

The door opened. I plopped back onto my chair, my hands behind me, and my ankles around the legs of the chair, the twine loose around them. Hopefully, no one would look too closely.

"He's coming," Sissy sang, entering the room. "This will all be over soon." She approached us. "Too bad your death won't be as creative as Daisy's. That one was my crowning glory."

"You're sick." I hoped ridiculing her would keep her from looking too closely at my feet.

"Shut up." She put her face close to mine. I smelled the coffee I bought on her breath. "You're going to be dead."

I swallowed against a suddenly dry mouth, trying to think of something clever and condescending to say. But, the reminder I might die soon, shoved all thoughts from my head.

The door opened again and Reed marched in.

25

"Well, if it isn't the two nosiest women in Oak Meadows." Reed grinned, his teeth startlingly white against his dark skin. "And so pretty, too. It's a pity, really, that I have to kill you."

"You don't have to kill us," I said. "You could just leave town."

He shook his head. "I will, but I don't leave behind those who know my business or betray me. Starr, pretending to be something she isn't, betrayed me. You, Miss Stormi, can't listen when warned."

"You are the biggest pretender." Linda spit it him.

He backhanded her across the face, then pulled a handkerchief from his pocket to wipe her blood from his knuckles. "I don't have the same rules, sweet girl."

He knelt in front of me and lifted the twine off the floor. "You've been busy."

I swallowed hard, then jumped to my feet, knocking him over.

Linda screamed, yanked against her restraints and also got to her feet.

I plunged my hand into my bra, pulled out my gun and tossed it to her. She shot Reed point blank in the chest before he was able to get to his feet. With the weapon pointed at Sissy, she calmly asked me to untie her ankles.

There was no way I could ever look at Linda as a young

high school student again. Her quick thinking had saved our lives. I hadn't done too shabby either. I got her feet free, then stood behind her.

"You killed him." Sissy fell to her knees beside the killer. She whipped a gun out of his pocket.

Before she could raise her arm, Linda laid her out beside Reed. She grabbed my arm. "Let's go. We can't take the chance that the rest of the gang isn't coming."

I nodded, cast one last look at the two people who tried to kill me, and jogged after my new best friend. At least for the moment. "Wait. My purse."

I dashed back into the room, grabbed my purse, and rushed to catch up with Linda. Where was Matt? I'd been missing at least an hour. Was Greta dead and unable to call for help? How long until my mother grew worried?

Outside, we sprinted for my jeep. "I'll drive." We had left the keys in the ignition, and Linda's hands looked painful. "You need medical attention."

"Give me your phone. I'll call Matt and have him meet us here. We can't take the chance that Reed's goons will come and remove the body."

"Um, I only have two bullets left in the gun."

"Why isn't the clip full?"

"I didn't think I would need more than that. I'm not a cop. I don't get into shoot outs."

Two cars sped into the parking lot and boxed us in. Two young men got out of each car and held semi-automatic weapons on us.

"Wonderful." Linda cursed.

I cringed at her language. I grabbed my phone from her hand and dialed Matt. "Where are you?"

"Where are you?" He asked in a teasing tone.

"About to get shot by gang members! Linda and I were tied up at a warehouse. Linda shot and killed Reed and Sissy.

Now, we're looking at four weapons aimed at my jeep." I started to cry.

"Whoa. Wait a minute. Where's Greta?"

"I think Sissy killed her when she hijacked me." I told him the approximate location of the warehouse.

"Keep your head down. We're coming!" Click.

"They're coming." I scooted down in the seat so that the doors covered me. Not that they would stop a bullet, but it made me feel better. "What do we do now?"

"Wait and hope no one gets an itchy trigger finger. Uh-oh."

"What?" I glared up at her. "Don't say uh-oh!"

"One of them is heading for the warehouse."

"They'll find Reed."

"That's why I said uh-oh. Get out of the jeep."

"Are you crazy?" I shook my head.

"We need to make it to that other building. I'll cover you."

I eyed the smaller building next to the larger warehouse. "We'll never make it with only two bullets."

"We have to try. Run in a low zig-zag pattern. The jeep will provide some protection. Wait for my go."

The man who had entered the warehouse, dashed out, shouting and waving his arms.

"Go!" Linda shoved me as the other three turned to face the yeller.

I ran as fast as I could, my gaze glued on the metal door with red chipped paint. Gunshots rang out. Linda returned fire. We banged through the door and slammed it behind us, throwing the deadbolt.

"Get out of sight." She dragged me into a small room. "Hopefully, we'll be safe here until help arrives."

"You're shot."

Blood seeped through her fingers. The stain spread across her side.

"It isn't bad." She slid to the floor.

"Don't lie." I glanced around what looked like an office. There had to be something I could use to stop the bleeding.

I found some paper napkins and pressed them against her side. "Hold this while I look around some more."

"You going to write about this in your next book?"

"Most likely. It will be a best seller don't you think?" I glanced at her paling face.

"Definitely. Make me out to be a hero, won't you?"

I found some hand towels, not the cleanest things, but better than nothing. I folded them into a square and removed my bra to tie them into place with.

"That's creative." Linda forced a smile.

"Writers are creative." I slid down the wall and sat on the floor beside her, waiting for Matt to arrive.

Sirens wailed outside. The gunfire increased.

When it grew silent, I stood and opened the door. Matt stood in the middle of the parking lot, turning in a slow circle. Three young men, writhed on the pavement as officers removed their weapons. One lay unmoving.

I sobbed and raced toward my love. "Matt!" I threw my arms around his neck.

He tightened his arms around me, kissing me, smoothing my hair, running his hands down my arms and back. "Are you okay?"

I nodded. "But Linda's been shot. She's in there." I pointed, then followed him as he called to paramedics waiting next to an ambulance. "Officer down!"

Within minutes, she was hooked to an IV and put in the back of the ambulance. She handed me my empty gun. "You're a strong woman, Stormi Nelson."

I nodded through my tears, more grateful for the young female cop than I could say. If not for her, I would have died.

Matt pulled his arm around my shoulder. "Let's go home."

"That's the second best thing I've heard in a long time." I leaned into him.

"What was the first?"

"When you said you loved me at the restaurant."

It was over. Who knew that a simple skincare party could have started all this? Skincare really could be murder. I was having no more of it. No lotions or potions were worth all this. Whatever new scheme Angela came up with to make money, I wanted no part of it.

Matt helped me into his car, placing a gentle kiss on my forehead. "You scare me."

"I scare myself. It's a good thing you're so wildly in love with me that you can overlook such things."

He laughed. "Yes, it is." I settled into the seat, secure in the fact that Matt would always find me, no matter where I was, no matter how someone tried to hurt me, he would be there. Always.

ABOUT THE AUTHOR

www.cynthiahickey.com

Cynthia Hickey is a multi-published and best-selling author of cozy mysteries and romantic suspense. She has taught writing at many conferences and small writing retreats. She and her husband run the publishing press, Winged Publications. They live in Arizona and Arkansas, becoming snowbirds with three dogs. They have ten grandchildren who keep them busy and tell everyone they know that "Nana is a writer."